RESCUE YOU

SYLVIE KURTZ

For all the dogs I've been lucky enough to know.
You've added love and laughter and an indescribable richness to my life.
Thank you!

TRIGGER WARNING

This story deals with a character going through episodes of PTSD.

AUTHOR'S NOTE

For story purposes, Caleb's recovery is faster than it would likely be in real life. Also, in my mind, Caleb is currently seeing a therapist.

"When we have the courage to walk into our story and own it, we get to write the ending. And when we don't own our stories of failure, setbacks, and hurt—they own us."

— BRENÉ BROWN

"You're not broken. You're hurt and in need of compassionate care."

— ARIELLE SCHWARTZ, *THE COMPLEX PTSD WORKBOOK*

1

———————

The loud *rat-a-tat* on the door roused me from a sleep riddled with snores and yips and low growls. I cracked an eye open and glanced at the clock above my desk. Six a.m. I groaned. Rae, my day helper, must have forgotten her key. Again. At least she'd shown up.

I tried to extricate myself from the pile of dogs who'd insisted on joining me on the narrow cot in my office when a thunderstorm had rolled through at 2 a.m. Sadie, the pit bull mix, had her snout tucked in my armpit. Hercules, the sausage dog, snaked his body alongside mine, his arthritic paw on my chest, his fish breath fanning my face. And Bubbles, the black-and-white mutt with three legs, had wound her body through my legs as if they were agility weave poles. Far away, the last rolls of thunder rumbled through the countryside.

"Up you go!" The dogs slowly released me in a concert of groans and snuffles and stretches. I unfolded from the cot, feeling every muscle in my body ache. This wasn't sustainable. If I was going to spend this many nights at the canine center, I needed a better bed. And maybe a real day off.

I padded to the door, the dogs racing ahead, barking, finally realizing they were falling down on their self-appointed job of protecting me.

"Rae ..." I pulled the front door open, making the bone-shaped "Welcome" sign rattle against the wood. Brisk, rain-freshened autumn air rushed in, making me wish I'd put on a sweatshirt over my t-shirt. "You've got to remember—"

But Rae didn't stand there, looking sheepish. Instead, a woman in a black business suit and a tight bun stood before me, a white West Highland terrier in her arms. Worry lines crimped the corners of her eyes and tugged at the sides of her mouth.

"Sorry to knock so early. But I saw your car and took a chance you'd be in." She tipped her chin toward the lobby. "Can I come in?"

"Sure." I opened the door, allowing her inside. She seemed to know me, but I had no idea who she was. This dog wasn't one of our regulars. I ran my fingers through my sleep-mussed hair and knotted the long strands into a messy bun, trying to look a bit more professional.

She set the terrier on the ground, red leash snaking from her hand, then slapped her free hand at the white hairs decorating her black jacket.

The terrier turned toward me and yipped, front feet coming off the ground with the sound. *"I don't belong here."*

Good to know, I silently told him.

My three foster dogs circled the terrier, sniffing him all over. The terrier growled. *"Nose off!"*

The woman knotted her hands in front of her. "I'm sorry to do this to you, but I didn't know what else to do. I can't keep him. He's not good with the kids. He nips at them and growls, and I'm afraid he's going to hurt one of them."

"They pull my tail. And ears. Hard. They steal my food. And the girl ... She puts clothes on me!"

I tried hard not to laugh at the terrier's outrage.

"So, you need daycare for him?" My center offered doggie daycare, boarding and training classes. "A series of obedience classes?"

"No, I can't have him in my house at all, and the shelter told me that if I returned him there, he'd be put to sleep. Apparently, it's his third strike." She shook her head. "I should've realized there was something wrong with him when the shelter manager told me that."

The terrier huffed. *"Nothing wrong with me. It's them. They're so loud!"*

I tried to concentrate on the woman's explanation, but the terrier's thoughts kept penetrating my mind, distracting me. *Shhh, you can fill me in later.*

"But the kids fell in love with him." She looked down at the terrier, standing stoic, surrounded by my sniffing dogs. "And he is awfully cute." She shook her head. "But so surly and disobedient. I think we're going to wait to get a dog until the kids are older." She pointed a finger at him. "And he needs a home without children."

The terrier sneezed. *"First good idea you've had."*

"So, you want me to take him?"

She sighed her relief. "Yes, please." She handed me the leash. "Just because he doesn't fit in our household, doesn't mean he wouldn't make someone else a good dog. I don't want him put to sleep just because of that, you know. I don't want that on my conscience."

I knew. That's how I'd ended up with three special-needs fosters. But I couldn't keep adding to my collection. I was already barely making ends meet. The overdue vet bill for Hercules's meds sat heavy on my mind. The center's rent was due in two days. And the food supply for the dogs was running dangerously low. Sadie required sensitive stomach feed, which wasn't cheap. I had only so many ways to stretch the dollars I managed to take in.

"And," the woman continued. "I heard through the grapevine that you save unsavable dogs."

"*Not going back there,*" the terrier barked.

I looked down at him. His tail twitched, an almost imperceptible wag that softened his defiance. I was a sucker when it came to dogs, especially when they looked so vulnerable. I firmly believed there were no bad dogs.

"Okay," I said to both. "I'll take him and see if I can find him a good home."

"Thank you, thank you, thank you." She reached into her jacket pocket and took out a check. "Here's a little something to help you with his care."

"Thank you. That's a big help." A bigger help than she realized. With that, I could support him for a month. That gave me time to find him the right home.

She nodded, then with a last look at the terrier, she turned to leave. "His name is Max, by the way." She smiled, a tight line with no mirth. "Maximus, because he thinks he's a big dog."

"*Hey!*" Max barked.

After the woman left, I took the three fosters into the play area out back, then returned to the lobby for a quick chat with Max. I'd have to get the morning chores started soon, because —I glanced at my watch—apparently, Rae wasn't going to show up. Again.

The helper situation was getting dire. I couldn't continue to work the place 24/7 alone. That wasn't sustainable either. I had to hope that Bo showed up at ten, or I'd have to bug Mom again to bring me food again and endure another lecture about finding reliable help. It wasn't as if I purposely hired undependable people; there just weren't that many people even willing to work at the center. And I couldn't afford to pay them as much as I wanted to, or they deserved. So, I was caught in one of those lovely catch-22s.

I sat cross-legged on the floor, inviting Max onto my lap.

He sat in front of me, chin in the air, refusing my offer.

I respected his boundaries. "Tell me your story."

"*I'm looking for someone.*" He sniffed the air as if that would help him find his person.

"Okay. Who?"

"*Don't know.*" He sniffed the air again. "*I got no breakfast.*"

"The quicker you tell me your story, the quicker I can feed you guys."

He harrumphed. "*Not much to say. The first house kicked me around. I bit the guy. He kicked me back hard. I ended up somewhere smelly. Got my ribs taped.*" He nipped at his ribs as if they still hurt. "*Then I ended up in an awful place. Too loud. Too many sad dogs.*" He plopped down. "*The second place forgot all about me. Spent all my time alone in the yard. So, I left.*" He shook his head as if he were trying to shake off something. "*Got trapped by the neck. Taken back to that awful place.*" He shivered. "*Then this family took me from there. I wanted to be good. But those kids.*" He sniffed the air. "*Do I smell bacon?*"

"No bacon."

"*I swear, I smell bacon.*"

"Probably the diner down the road."

"*I could use some bacon.*"

"I'm going to have to find you a home." And with everything else I had going on right now, that wasn't going to be easy. I could add him to the slate of dogs at the adoption booth at the upcoming Pumpkin Festival Adopt-a-Thon. I did have my fosters up on my website as possible adoptees, so I could add him there, too. "But I can't do that unless you behave."

"*I told you. I'm looking for someone.*"

I reached out and scratched him under the chin. He leaned into my hand. Not a bad dog at all. Just one that hadn't found the proper home. Yet. "But if you can't tell me who, I can't help you look for them."

He snuffled. "*I'll know 'em when I see 'em.*"

I sighed. Sometimes, you had to know when to give. I had a month to find him a good home. "Okay, let's get some breakfast."

He hopped up, tail wagging. "*Now you're talkin'.*"

Max trailed me to the small equipment room where I kept the boarders' food and a Vittles Vault of kibble for the fosters. I'd barely untwisted the lid when Max hopped up, burying his head in the container.

"Max!" I hauled him back, but he wriggled like a fish on a line. His unrelenting determination was as maddening as it was impressive.

"Hungry!" He barked, tail wagging like a flag on top of Mount Washington—the windiest peak in the U.S.

I finally managed to pull him off and scooped a portion of food into a bowl. While I prepared meals for the other dogs, Max devoured his breakfast. His hunger was more than physical. It had a desperation I understood only too well—a gnawing need to prove he belonged, to fight for the scraps in a world that seemed to tell him he wasn't worth the trouble.

"What am I going to do with you?" I whispered.

Max paused mid-chew, glancing up at me with an expression so raw, so unexpectedly vulnerable that it caught me off guard. The defiance in his eyes softened and, just for a moment, I saw hope, fragile and fleeting.

I leaned against the counter, arms folded, as he licked the bowl clean. "You don't make things easy for yourself, do you?"

Max paused, looking up at me, beard filled with kibble crumbs. "*Got a mission.*"

"A mission?"

But he didn't answer, just went back to licking the already spotless dish. I shook my head, a reluctant smile tugging at my lips.

"All right, buddy." I crouched down beside him, my hand reaching out to scratch behind his ears. "We're in this together for now. But if we're going to make this work, you're going to have to meet me halfway."

Max tilted his head.

"Deal?" I offered him a hand.

He lifted a paw and placed it in my palm. The gesture a promise.

"Let's get the rest of the gang fed."

Maybe I couldn't fix him overnight. Maybe he'd drive me crazy. But as Max fell into step behind me, I realized he hadn't given up. He was still looking for his place.

And maybe that was enough to start.

2

───────

By ten, the morning chores were done. The two overnight boarders, the half-dozen daycare dogs and the three—make that four with Max—fosters were happily playing in one of two areas: small dogs in one pen; big dogs in the other. At least Bo had called. He was running late, but he'd get here soon. I finally had a minute to call Mom.

"Ah, Lark." Mom tutted at my request for food and clean clothes. "I know this center is your passion project but there's got to be a better way to make a living. You're running yourself ragged working all those hours. Plus getting ready for the Adopt-a-Thon." She clucked. "You're not doing yourself or the dogs any good."

"Mom, please, no lecture. The dogs need a safe place, and I give it to them. As for the Adopt-a-Thon, who better to advocate for the dogs than someone who gets them?" I was getting myself worked up and needed to take it down a notch. *Deep breath.* "Like I said, if you're coming this way, I could use some food. And a change of clothes."

I'd spent the last three days here without a break. What I really needed was a shower before my ripeness scared the customers away. Maybe I could see how much it would cost to add one. I snorted. *Yeah, with what extra cash?*

Mom sighed. "Give me half an hour."

MOM AND BO arrived at the same time, which allowed me the chance to eat lunch at the desk in my office while Bo supervised the dog play areas. The dogs loved his golden retriever-like energy and his willingness to play endless games.

Mom unpacked a feast of sandwiches, fruit salad and chocolate chip cookies, along with a thermos of coffee. My brain sighed in gratitude at the caffeine. The sweet scent of chocolate made me remember the old days when I used to bake with Mom—before life got so complicated. My stomach grumbled at the sight of the food, but I barely had the energy to enjoy it.

"How's the Adopt-a-Thon coming along?" Mom picked at the crust of a turkey sandwich. Her eyes flickered to the door and the play area where Bo tossed a Frisbee to a black Lab, who jumped up to catch it with a happy bark, but her focus was elsewhere.

"We still need more donations for the silent auction, but otherwise it's coming along. Phoebe's supposed to stop by sometime today to go over the to-do list." The Adopt-a-Thon was three weeks away, and we hoped to get at least a dozen shelter dogs adopted.

Phoebe Flowers managed the Tri-Town Dog Shelter, and after a summer of adoptions, the shelter found itself crowded again now that school had started. The three towns who helped support the shelter tried to keep it a no-kill shelter, but when the space got overcrowded, the old and infirm were sometimes sacrificed to give the younger dogs a chance to find a forever home. That made Phoebe sick, so her Type-A personality worked relentlessly to find all dogs a home, any home. On that point, we differed. I felt the dogs needed the right home.

"Did you hit Aunt Grace for a donation?" Mom tucked a piece of lettuce back into her sandwich.

Aunt Grace ran the local Wash 'n Wags shop where you could bathe your dog and buy all sorts of locally made dog equipment. "She's donating a collar and leash to each adopted dog as well as a bath coupon."

But Mom didn't respond. She seemed lost in her own thoughts, picking at the sandwich bread, but not eating anything.

"Something on your mind?" I took another big bite of sandwich. My stomach felt tight, and I had to swallow hard to get the bite down. Something was definitely up. Our semi-regular conversations about getting a "real" job had put distance between us over the past few years. My hunger disappeared, but I forced myself to keep eating, not knowing when I'd get to eat again.

"I'm deliberating," Mom said.

"About?"

She took in a big breath, then blew it out. Her fingers worked as if she were trying to crochet her paper napkin into one of her arts-and-crafts projects. She was nervous, more than just her regular Mom-trying-to-fix-things. The words seemed to require force to take shape. I braced myself against her carefully couched criticism. When the words finally burst out, catching their meaning took me a second.

"Aimee is back in town."

Not what I expected at all.

"Oh." The bite of sandwich landed like a wad of wet concrete in my stomach. I pushed the half-eaten sandwich back on its waxed paper cover and sat back in my chair, feeling the room close in on me. The playful barks in the play area became muted as though my ears had filled with cotton.

I wasn't going to ask what Aimee was doing back in Brighton. I wasn't going to give her any of my thoughts. Not after what she'd done.

"She's married now." Mom's gaze searched my face for a reaction.

"Good for her." I sprang up and tidied my desk, stuffing the fruit salad and half sandwich into the mini fridge. I grabbed the empty coffee mug, accidentally clinking it against the side of the desk, then didn't know what to do with it. My body was too tense to move, too restless to stay still. Memories I didn't want to remember crowded in—of Aimee, of our friendship, of her betrayal—but I shook them away. "I should get back to work."

"She wants to apologize, Lark. To reconnect."

"Too late." The words spewed, raw and bruised. The time for that would've been twelve years ago in high school when she betrayed my trust. No, not betrayed, *shattered*. A sharp pain split through my chest, and I knuckled it away.

"Lark ..." Mom tipped her head to her shoulder, softened her voice. "Don't you think it's been long enough? You used to be best friends."

"Best friends don't do what she did to me. She ruined my life."

"That's an exaggeration."

"Do you really think so?" I spread my arms wide, voice rising despite myself. "Look around you." The pieces of my broken heart cracked even more. "I don't have any human friends. Just dogs."

"That's a choice you made."

"There was no choice. I was ridiculed and ostracized. Nobody wanted to stay around me." Somewhere in the play area, a dog whined. "I can't be myself with anybody. Not even with you, because even you don't want to hear about the dogs talking to me."

I knocked the coffee mug against the desktop, fingers

hanging on to the handle as if the ceramic was the only thing tethering me in place. "I had to leave Brighton to find some space where fewer people knew of my ability to talk to dogs. Do you know what it's like to be called crazy and weird and have people avoid you for something you can't even help?"

I'd accepted the opportunity to take over the Canine Center because it was in Stoneley. I would've gone farther away, except that I liked my family, liked spending time with them. And my twin brother, Liam, had already broken Mom's heart by choosing to stay in Europe after his stint in the army.

My free arm moved as if it were manned by a manic puppeteer. "When I got my dog training certification, I was told to never mention my ability, or I'd never be taken seriously."

The words had stung then, still stung now, but even they were nothing compared to the ache festering in me. Not good enough. Never good enough.

"I see how hard you've worked." Mom's eyes narrowed as if in pain, a crack in her powerful mom-armor. "I know it's been painful. I've never known how to help you." She thought she'd failed me back then when the gift to talk to dogs showed up when I was six, and later when the whole Aimee situation turned into a living nightmare in high school. "But people change, grow up."

"Not in my experience. Aimee's in the past and that's where she needs to stay." I moved toward the office door, but froze mid-step, a thought seizing me. My chest tightened, shallowing my breath. I had spent so many years rebuilding myself, finding a way to make peace with my gift—my curse—to serve the dogs who needed my help. But every day was also a reminder of what I'd lost. And right now, I wanted to feel anything but this hollow ache. I wanted the noise and the happy madness of the dogs in the play area. I wanted dog kisses and cuddles. "Thanks for the food. I appreciate you stopping by."

Max padded over and nudged my hand as if he sensed the

storm in me. I crouched down, stroking his soft hair. I squeezed my eyes shut. The dogs wanted me. They needed me. That was enough. I was enough. "What are you doing here?"

Bo came running up. "Sorry, the bugger's a little escape artist. He worked the latch!"

"*Not that hard,*" Max woofed.

You're too smart for your own good, I told him.

Bo scooped up Max and carried him back to the play area.

"About Aimee—" Mom handed me a tote bag with a change of clothes.

"I can't, Mom. I just can't." My voice cracked as I stood. Not after everything she'd done. I took the tote bag from Mom and pressed it to my chest, feeling the hard knocks of my heart against the denim of the bag.

Mom didn't say anything, but her eyes filled with sadness. "All I've ever wanted was for you to be happy."

"I know."

But wanting wasn't enough.

3

____

The dogs and the two private training classes I had that afternoon kept me too busy to think about Aimee and her return to Brighton. Reconnect. Pah. As if it was that easy. Did she not realize she'd ruined my life? I couldn't just sweep *that* under the carpet and be BFFs again as if nothing had happened. She had some nerve.

She didn't even have the guts to come to me herself but had gone through my mother. Not that I'd have welcomed her in. But still. That was the chicken's way out.

Before the stew of anger and resentment grew too heated, Phoebe Flowers blew through the center's front door like a northern wind, carrying her usual crackle of electricity. That impression of intense energy followed in the brisk movement of her limbs, the Medusa-like writhing of her dark curls and her rapid-fire speech.

She plopped a binder and a bag of Chinese take-out on the counter. "Figured you might not have eaten all day, so—"

"Thanks."

"Let's get down to business." She opened the binder and took out mug shots of twelve dogs. "There's only a couple of puppies this year. The rest are all older, post-Covid rejects who did nothing wrong except outgrow the work-from-home order."

I got paper plates from a cupboard in my office. The savory scent of sesame chicken, spring rolls and fried rice made my stomach growl. I hadn't eaten anything since that half sandwich this morning. Mom was right. I needed to take better care of myself, or I wouldn't do the dogs any good. "Those photos aren't doing the dogs any favor."

"That's all I got." She shuffled and reshuffled the photos as if a different order would give her different results. "Can't exactly call up a photographer for glamour shots now, can I?"

"Why not?" I grabbed a spring roll and nearly moaned as I bit through the shell. "I'll bet someone would be willing to make these dogs look good." Too bad Claire Chandler wasn't around these days. She would gladly have taken the job and done it for free. Last I heard, she and her husband were in Canada somewhere, Hunter writing his latest novel; Claire taking spectacular shots of rare birds.

Phoebe took the stack of photos and pushed it toward me. "Okay, then, that's yours." She turned a tab to a checklist. "How are the Brighton donations coming along?"

Phoebe had the task of cold-calling Stoneley businesses for donations either to the adoption goodie bags or for the silent auction to raise funds for the shelter. I got Brighton. Which, really, wasn't that bad, because of all the family I had living there.

"The Feed & Seed is donating a bag of dog food to each adoptee. Dr. Schafer is donating spaying or neutering as well as a check-up. The Blue Lotus studio is donating a month of yoga classes. The Brightside Bakery dog cookies for the bags and a basket for the auction. All the restaurants have donated dinner date coupons. Wintercrest, a weekend getaway. The Purple Page, a basket of books." I consulted my list that went on for two pages. "Just about every business in Brighton gave something. Chocolates, jams and jellies, cider, puzzles, a glass sculpture, a quilt, a dog paw necklace, soaps—"

"That's all good, but we need something big. Something that would say, 'look at me.' Something people would bid a lot of money on." Phoebe dug into a container of fried rice as if it were an archeological dig and she was unearthing an idol. "The shelter's not doing great. We need to refill the coffers before winter. Winter's always tough. The last thing I want is to have to close the shelter." She shoveled rice into her mouth and chewed like a motor. I doubted she tasted anything. "What would happen to the dogs?"

The shelter needed to stay open. Nothing else was acceptable. "We're doing great, and we still have almost three weeks to go." We had a lot of promised donations, but Phoebe was right. All of it was mostly small items. The small items would add up. But having something big to draw attention ... that would definitely help. "What did you have in mind for the big-bid item?"

Phoebe blew out a breath, stabbed the chopsticks back into the rice container. "I don't know. Something special." Her arms went wide, stirring the air as if she could manifest something out of thin air by sheer will. "Something extraordinary. Something—"

From the play area came Max's bark. "*Not going back! Not going back!*"

Phoebe frowned. "I know that bark."

Before I could stop her, she marched toward the play area. I stuffed what was left of my spring roll into my mouth, chewing as I raced after her.

Her lips pinched tight. "What's Max the Terrible doing here?"

Feeling protective of Max, I stepped into the play area. Max came bounding to me. "*Not going back there.*"

I crouched and petted him. *I'm not going to let anyone take you to the shelter.* "Everything's fine, Max."

"Better if you got her outta here," Max barked.

She's here to help me help you.

"Heard that before."

"His owner didn't want to bring him back to the shelter." I let Max crawl into my lap. "And he's not terrible. He's just misunderstood."

"He's marked." She shook a finger at me. "You make sure you find him a home because he can't come back to the shelter. Ever."

"So I heard."

Max pressed closer to me, his small body trembling. *You're safe here, Max. I promise.*

"I know." I petted the top of Max's head. "I plan on finding him a good home."

Max was still young and trainable, so finding him a home should be easier than for a senior dog with arthritis, a three-legged dog, or a dog with PTSD.

"I hope so." With that, Phoebe sighed and trekked back to her file.

I pushed Max toward Bubbles, who was waiting, tail wagging to play with him, then went back to the lobby.

Phoebe focused on her list once again. "How's the adoption booth construction coming along?"

"Aaron assured me it would be done in time." My cousin was a master carpenter and an all-around good guy. He and his wife had gotten Amber, a Cavalier King Charles puppy, from Lizzie's last litter. That puppy had brought them together—as I knew she would. Amber was now a doting big sister to the twins Aaron and Merry adopted last summer. My heart ached at the thought of my beautiful dog. I still couldn't believe Queen Elizabeth of Brighton, my Lizzie, was gone, that one unexpected fever had taken her from healthy to heaven in just a few days.

"He's building three rings." I forced myself back to the

conversation. "One for bigger dogs, one for smaller dogs and one for the puppies. The booth will house the baskets for the silent auction, information pamphlets, and—"

"We need something fun, something interactive." Phoebe tapped her front teeth with the end of her pen. "Something that will bring people in."

"The dogs should be enough. Everyone loves dogs."

"But we need them to stay for more than a pat. We need them to stay so we can talk to them, show them how great the dogs are. Make them take one home."

"We need the *right* people to take them home, or they'll just bounce back. And that won't do you any good."

Phoebe's expression hardened, her voice edging with frustration. "You don't get it. We don't have time to be picky. We're drowning, Lark, and that means putting some dogs to sleep or closing down permanently. I don't want to do either. I *need* these dogs adopted."

"Throwing dogs at the first person who shows interest isn't a solution. It's just setting the new owners and the dogs up for heartbreak."

She threw up her hands. "You think I don't know that? But we don't have the luxury of perfect. We need numbers—adoptions, donations—whatever it takes to keep dogs alive and the doors open."

The tension in the room thickened, turning my breath shallow. Before I could respond, Phoebe scribbled something on her list and changed gear. "What about big-ticket donors? Have you hit Brighton's deep pockets yet?"

I hesitated. Yes, Brighton had its share of wealthy residents, but asking for big money wasn't my strength. What Phoebe didn't realize was that my connections were with the working people of Brighton, not the people with deep pockets. "You're better at it."

"My plate's already full, so the ball's in your court."

"I'm working on it."

"Working on it? We don't have time for 'working on it.'" She drilled her pen tip against the counter, leaving ink marks on the wood. "I heard through the grapevine that someone bought the Thorned Bough vineyard. They're supposedly loaded, and word is they're generous for causes they believe in. Make them believe in ours."

They'd have to be loaded to fix up the place. The previous owner—a divorcing couple—had fought a hard battle over ownership and the rights to the wine while the house and land sat idle for years. In the end, the bank had sold it when neither the wife, nor the husband stepped up to pay the massive debts the vineyard had accumulated. "Do you know who bought the place?"

"No idea. I heard he's new money from down south but likes to keep a low profile. Heard he had ties to Brighton."

Ties to Brighton? That could fit a few people who'd come back to town this year—like Caleb Singer, who was taking over his father's store and the Swann sisters, who were updating their father's cidery. And Aimee. Last I heard, she was into art restoration, not making wine. I shook my head. *Not gonna think about Aimee or why she's in Brighton.*

Mom would know who'd bought the place. She knew everything that happened in town. "I'll look into it."

"What about the Swann sisters over at The Cidery? They could give a wedding package."

"They already gave a basket of ciders. I happen to know that they're running on a thin margin right now as they're rebuilding the business since their father passed."

"Aren't we all running on a thread? You don't get anything unless you ask. And they can place restrictions, like good only for their slow time of the year, so it wouldn't really cost them anything."

"Fine." I gritted my teeth. "I'll ask."

"Perfect. Let's make it happen." Phoebe's expression softened for just a moment. "The shelter's counting on you. If we can land something big, it could save us."

Max let out a playful bark, his head popping up over the play area's waist-high wall. Phoebe glanced at him. "You're going to have a hard time getting him adopted with his bad reputation."

"I've got it," I said more tightly than I intended, mostly because doubts crept in like shadows. What if I couldn't find the right home for him? I couldn't keep him either. I already had too many dogs depending on me.

Phoebe sighed, her energy deflating for the first time. "Sorry. I know I'm pushing, but this matters. I'm scared for the shelter." Her chin pointed toward the play area. "And for dogs like Max and your fosters who needs extra time, attention and training."

Phoebe added a jagged note to her list. "We need to empty out the shelter. Dogs are already sharing runs."

"I didn't realize it had gotten so bad."

Her brows furrowed. "I'm worried."

Just the thought of these rejected and scared dogs made me want to cry. "I was thinking about writing a story for each dog." Of asking each dog for their story, so it could attract the right person. "Something that would stir up emotions and make people want to adopt."

Phoebe's mouth flattened. "Um, yeah, sure. But we need more. Maybe you could do an agility demonstration. Or a puppy class."

"Good idea! There's a couple of dogs I trained I could call in for a demo." Maybe I would have time to teach Bubbles a couple of new tricks, tricks that would show that missing one leg wasn't holding her back in any way. "And I could take the puppies we have through a class to show people how fun it can be."

But Phoebe had stopped listening and moved on to the next item on her list. "We also need to ask Allegra to make sure there's a dedicated potty area for the dogs."

Allegra Livingstone Sheridan had taken over running the Candlewick Estate when the earl died. She was also the town administrator, in charge of all of Brighton's festivals. "On my to-do list."

Phoebe ran through her list of tasks, barely allowing me a word in. When she slammed her binder shut, the crack sounded final.

"We'll make this work," she said, more to herself than me.

She left with the same bluster with which she'd arrived, making the door slam behind her and the "Welcome" sign rattle.

I locked the door and headed toward the dogs.

"Talking to strangers." I reached out to pat Max, who stopped jumping. "Generous, anonymous, and tied to one of the fanciest estates in town."

"*Can't be any worse than talking to dogs,*" Max woofed.

"Dogs are easier."

"*'Course.*"

"Finding this mysterious donor is just the beginning. Then I have to convince him that dogs like you are worth parting with his money."

"*No problem. I can turn on the tricks.*" Max ran through his bag of tricks—sit pretty, high five, spin, rollover and prayer pose—making me laugh.

Squeezing money out of someone who just bought a money pit would take more than Max's charm. He did have a point, though. Taking a dog with me would both give me courage and show what was at stake.

I put the dogs to bed and ran through my nighttime check-list, making sure everyone had a last trip outside and were nice and comfy in their sleep quarters. Max had dogged my every footstep as if he were afraid to lose sight of me.

And as Kari, my three-times-a-week night helper arrived, I sighed my relief. Finally, a break—warm food, a hot shower and a bed all to myself. Of course, the last part was kind of sad.

"Got a big test to study for." Kari dumped her Bohemian-patterned backpack at her feet in front of the reception desk. It landed with a thud of heavy books. She was a small woman, who looked like a pre-teen even though she was in her mid-twenties. She caught sight of Max, and a wide smile took over her face. "Who's this charming fellow?"

"Your study buddy. His name is Max." I narrowed my gaze at Max. "And he's an escape artist, so you'll have to keep an eye on him."

"Good, I need someone to keep me awake. Got any coffee?"

"Bo brought fresh supplies."

She brought her palms together in front of her heart. "Thank you, Bo."

"All right." I grabbed my own battered backpack and Mom's tote with my dirty clothes. "I'll be back in the morning."

As I drove home, I couldn't shake the bad feeling roiling in my gut about the Thorned Bough vineyard and its mysterious new owner.

4

———————

The next afternoon, while Rae kept the daycare dogs busy, I got a chance to take a break. Outside, wind whipped at the red maple leaves, brown oak leaves and yellow beech leaves, stirring them into a confetti froth that fell to the ground. The sky had turned an angry gray. Rain wasn't far off.

I had just settled at my desk to update the center's website with Max's information, when Max barked out. *"He's here! He's here!"*

I went to the play area where Rae ran the big dogs through a series of obstacles she'd put together for their entertainment. Max, at the small-pen door, jumped up with each bark. *"He's here! He's here!"*

I reached down to pet Max. *Who's here?*

He hopped out of my reach, bouncing like a drop of water in hot oil. *"Him! My guy!"*

There's no one here other than me and Rae.

At that moment, the front door blew open, letting in a skitter of leaves. A man, bent over against the wind, pushed in, silver reflective jacket, gloves and bicycle helmet making him look like some sort of alien creature. The air in the room seemed to shift, charged with the sudden energy of his arrival, as though he'd brought the storm inside with him. Outside, a crack of thunder rumbled through the countryside.

"*Told ya*," Max barked.

I hurried to the lobby. The man took off his helmet and shook his head. His gaze circled the room, taking in the dog photographs along the walls, going right over me as if I weren't there. He swept away a fall of shaggy dark brown hair from his eyes with a hand. I gasped. The gesture was both familiar and strangely stiff.

I recognized him, of course. I'd spent most of my childhood running after my brother Liam and his best friend Caleb Singer. For a while in elementary school, my mother had referred to us as the three musketeers. But Caleb looked nothing like I remembered. Gone was the teasing light of mischief in his eyes, the cool swagger of his steps, the ooze of confidence. Now his whole body gave a vibe of hyper vigilance and pain as if it were a frayed rope about to snap.

"Hi, there." I stepped behind the reception counter, my voice coming out more tartly than I intended. "Can I help you?"

He placed his helmet on the wooden bench by the door. "Your website said you have dogs for adoption."

"Why come here?" I tried not to sound defensive. "Why not the shelter where you'd have more choices?"

He shrugged concentrating on the photographs of playing dogs on the wall. "Too noisy."

Did he not recognize me? Had he not seen my name on the website? He'd left Brighton right after high school, choosing to attend college in Washington state—as far away as he could get. Though he'd changed, I pretty much hadn't. *Hey*, I wanted to say. *Remember me?* But the slump of his shoulders warned me to keep my distance. "Right now, I have four fosters."

He looked right at me, but no flash of recognition entered

his eyes. Maybe the rumors were true. Some had him nearly dying and coming home to heal after some sort of accident. Broken inside, if not out. But his father told anyone who'd listen that his youngest son had finally seen the light and come home to take over the Country Store, so Lionel could retire.

I led him to the play area where the fosters and daycare dogs played with their usual gusto, but I didn't have a good feeling about adoption. None of the dogs were right for a guy healing from trauma. "The dachshund in the corner is nine and has arthritis."

"That's not going to work."

"*Pick me! Pick me!*" Max barked, parking himself right by Caleb on the other side of the waist-high wall.

"The pit bull mix—" I started.

He nodded once. "I'll take that one."

"She has a delicate stomach and is dealing with canine PTSD."

"Okay."

I hesitated, not knowing for sure what his problem was. "I really don't think she's the one for you. Two of you dealing with PTSD—"

"Who says I have PTSD?" His voice tightened, lending a sharp edge to his words.

"*I can help!*" Max wagged his tail so hard, his whole body vibrated.

I couldn't exactly tell Caleb that it screamed from him as brightly as his cycling gear with his twitching fingers and itchy feet and hollow eyes. Or that Max knew he needed help. Most people thought I was crazy when I told them dogs could talk to me. And Caleb and Liam had led the name-calling parade in middle school, then joined in for another round in high school. I'd learned to keep quiet and hadn't mentioned my ability in over a decade.

"It's a recipe for disaster," I said, softening my tone. "She needs more support than you could give her."

"And you're an expert on me?"

"No, on her. On dogs." I turned away from his piercing gaze, heat rising up my neck. "You're not my first." That came out wrong. Of course, Caleb had always had a way of making me tongue-tied.

"Well, that got personal fast." His gaze returned to the dog pens, his whole body still defensive.

"I've trained service dogs for people with PTSD before is what I meant."

He gave one sharp nod. "What do you suggest?"

"Of all my dogs, Max would be the best for you." Although I wasn't sure that was true. Not if he followed his track record of defiance and running away. I opened the door to the pen and invited Caleb through.

"About time." Max parked his butt in front of Caleb, tail sweeping madly behind him, and tapped at his knee with a paw. *"Down here, Bud."*

Caleb glanced down at Max, who wagged his whole body in unadulterated joy. For a moment something softened in Caleb's expression. It left as quickly as it had come. He clenched his fists and unclenched them as if he were trying to wring the tension out of his skin.

"Let's go," Max barked.

Caleb crossed his arms in front of his chest. "You're kidding."

"There's more to Max than appears. He's—"

Caleb's hands made an invisible box around Max's shape. "Look at him."

"His size bothers you?"

Caleb huffed. "What is he, like ten pounds?"

"More like fifteen."

"Small but mighty," Max barked.

"How is a dog the size of a football going to help when ..."

"A trigger hits?"

Caleb gave a curt nod. "And all that barking. That won't work either."

Outside, a sudden gust of rain lashed at the windows like a fist demanding inside. Sadie whined. Eyes wild, Bubbles ran in circles, looking for a place to hide. Hercules howled. A prong of lightning made the room glow like midday. A crack of thunder followed. The power shorted, throwing the room into shades of gray. The rest of the dogs joined the concert with barks. Rae worked to corral and calm down the dogs.

Caleb froze and fell to his knees, skin whiter than death, breath thin as a straw, eyes vacant.

Max climbed onto Caleb's lap and pressed his little body hard against Caleb's torso. "*I got ya, Bud. I got ya.*"

Max nuzzled Caleb's hand, his small frame seeming to take in the squall of Caleb's emotions.

The power flicked back on.

Caleb's breath returned to normal, his pulse slowed. His face remained impassive as he glanced at Max and slowly stroked the dog's head. Just as quickly, his expression hardened. He pushed Max off his lap and got up. He spun on the heel of his boot, then left without a word.

"*Hey!*" Max barked, running after Caleb, the pen door stopping him when Caleb slammed it behind him. "*What about me?*"

What exactly had happened? Was thunder a trigger? If so, what was he doing out in weather like this? Why hadn't he waited for a sunny day to come in? "Doesn't look like it'll happen today, Max."

"*Take me to him!*"

"I can't do that." He wouldn't hear anything right now. Too much shame existed when it came to men showing emotions or any sign of weakness. And Caleb was never one to let his fear show. Not the way his two older brothers teased him about being a wuss while growing up.

Max scratched at the door with both front paws. "*Let me out! Let me out!*"

At the front door, Caleb paused mid-step, hand on the doorknob. For a moment, I thought he might turn around, but he straightened, his jaw tightening.

He grabbed his helmet, hesitated, and glanced back at Max jumping up in the pen, still barking at him. Frown deepening, he put on his helmet and hunched against the wind and rain. Lightning cracked, illuminating Caleb as he stepped outside, his expression savage, an echo of everything going on inside him—restlessness, unpredictability and something about to break wide open. Not in a good way.

What exactly had happened to him?

"*My guy.*" Max whined, a pitiful sound that arrowed straight into my heart and made me think I'd been wrong about him. He did have a mission, and he knew what it was.

And it seemed it was Caleb.

Max had managed to calm Caleb down. Something I hadn't expected, given his ornery reputation. That was something. And his fierce loyalty to a man he didn't know had to count for something, too.

If they did belong together, forcing the issue right now would just make Caleb balk more. I needed to *show* him that he and Max belonged together. "We need to come up with a plan that'll show him that you're his guy."

Lightning forked the sky, but thunder didn't follow—as if the countryside was holding its breath for whatever came next.

5

———

I'd come to the center early the next morning to prepare for my visit to Thorned Bough vineyard. I'd tossed and turned all night, trying to come up with a plan, the perfect talking points, the best story to win over this mysterious owner's heart. I put together a portfolio of photos of dogs and the shelter's crowded runs. Would that be enough for him to open his wallet and help the shelter?

I'd thought about bringing Max with me, because even though he was ornery, he was also awfully cute. Cuteness tended to melt hearts. But Max had made it clear he wanted Caleb, and I couldn't risk he'd misbehave just to prove his point, costing me a much-needed donation.

I decided to take Bubbles instead. As her name implied, she had a bubbly personality and energy to spare, even with three legs. Her border collie half made her fast and her poodle half made her too smart for her own good. A big vineyard to run around in might just prove the perfect place for her. A wealthy owner would ensure she'd get all the care she needed.

I led Bubbles to the bathroom I'd converted to a dog

grooming room. "Play your card right, and you may have a new home by nightfall."

Bubbles wagged her tail. "*Home.*"

"Mom said this Oliver Gaines has a soft spot for causes like the shelter." I lifted Bubbles onto the grooming table.

I brushed the tangles out of her black-and-white coat. "You be your cutest self today, okay?"

"*Good girl,*" Bubbles woofed.

Not a judgment, just a statement of fact. She was a good girl, even if she didn't understand the meaning of good. I gave her a kiss on the head. "Yes, you are."

So, I gave her a bath and a blowout, making sure she looked as good as she could. I added a bandana sprinkled with hearts to her collar. She looked adorable. Then I put on a bright pink harness that fit her outgoing personality. "What do you think?"

"Woof!"

"You are beautiful."

"*Good girl,*" she woofed.

"The best."

As I'd bathed Bubbles, daycare dogs had come in. Their cheerful barking from the play area and the framed photographs of happy dogs on the sunshine-colored walls around the lobby usually warmed my heart. They were my success stories. Making dogs happy was the reason I'd accepted running the center. Today, the photographs were a reminder of everything that was at stake, especially for the fosters.

I clipped a leash to Bubbles' harness. "Ready?"

She lifted a paw and barked. "*Yes, yes, yes!*"

I was reaching for my jacket and purse when Mr. Pitt, the center's landlord, shuffled through the door, his ebony cane thunking on the wood floor with each step. Sparse gray hair, neat and tidy, covered a shiny skull. He wore an unbuttoned black trench coat. Beneath, he had on a black suit jacket, a gray shirt and a tie in shades of gray. Natty, Grandma would have called him.

More like slick, I thought.

"Hello, Lark." He smiled but instead of putting me at ease, it reminded me of Hannibal Lecter in the movie *Silence of the Lambs* when he said, "I ate his liver with some fava beans and a nice chianti." As tweens, Aimee and I had scared ourselves silly, watching that movie alone one night at her house. I shook the memory out of my head.

Bubbles growled. I crouched down beside her and petted her side. She pressed into me.

"Hi, Mr. Pitt." I tried to find a welcoming smile but couldn't. His being here couldn't be good. He always made me come to him. "I was going to drop the rent check off to your office later this afternoon."

"Yes, thank you. Your promptness is always appreciated." Another smile that didn't inspire confidence. "That is actually why I dropped by. I wanted to inform you in person that I will not be renewing your lease."

"What?" My heart took a tumble. Sensing my tension, Bubbles shifted and whined. "Why?"

He tipped his head as if what he'd just said wasn't a life-changing bit of news. "I got an offer I couldn't refuse for the land. And my wife has been after me to retire and move to North Carolina so she can be closer to her sisters."

I rose, holding on to Bubbles' leash. "What if I make you an offer?"

He laughed, a dry, sinister sound. "I know how much you make running this place. You cannot afford a counteroffer."

He named a sum that made my heart sink. Definitely out of my price range even if I threw in my life savings, which didn't amount to much to start with. "Why would they offer you so much?"

"Luxury condos. They'll rake in thousands a month in rent

per unit. You know how it is." He tapped the end of his cane on the floor. "Location, location, location, my dear. Close to ski country. That's why I'm selling while I can."

"But the dogs ... they depend on this place." I tried to keep my voice from shaking. So many people depended on the center to keep their dogs safe and happy during the day while they were at work. Safe and happy while they took a vacation. Safe and happy during the training sessions that made them better companions. "Don't you see how much it matters to the people who need a safe haven for their pets?"

He tutted, as if he were dealing with a child. "It's a charming little operation, I'll grant you that. But it's not my problem. I run a business, not a charity. You should have prepared for a possible exit, especially given your tenancy-at-will lease."

"We can't just shut down overnight." My thoughts spun in a whirlwind of worries. How? What if ...? "Will you give me the chance to find out if I can get a loan?"

His gray eyebrows, low over his eyes, pinched together. "I very much doubt any bank will advance you a loan."

"I won't know unless I try." My chin rose.

"I'm sorry, but I have already accepted the offer."

I swallowed hard, thinking of everything I would need to do to find a suitable replacement and keep the center going. Tears tightened my throat, but I swallowed them down. "How long can we stay?"

"I need you out by the end of the month," Mr. Pitt said, and I couldn't detect an ounce of regret.

"That's not going to be enough to find a suitable building *and* have it fitted for the dogs."

Bubbles whined again. I petted her head, and she licked my hand.

"Alas, that is not my problem. The buyer wants to take possession on November 1st. The building is set to be demolished on the fifteenth. He would like to break ground on those condos before winter."

Demolished? All the work I'd put in to create this safe haven for the dogs, reduced to rubble in less than a day. I placed a hand on my stomach, hoping my breakfast would stay down. "This isn't fair."

"Fair doesn't pay the bills." Mr. Pitt tsked. "This isn't personal, Lark. I like you. I really do. It's simply business."

I nodded, biting the inside of my cheek to keep from crying. The man had no compassion. "I'll figure something out," I mumbled, my grip tightening around the leash.

"You're welcome to try." He shrugged and turned to leave. "Good luck."

The door shut with a dismissive thwack behind him, leaving me standing in the middle of the cheerful lobby. The photographs on the yellow walls. All those happy dogs. They seemed to taunt me now.

Loser. Weirdo. Crazy. The long-ago jeers came back to haunt me.

Not the same, I told myself.

This operation had always run on a shoestring. I tried to keep prices reasonable to help as many dogs as possible. But maybe I'd shot myself in the foot by doing that. If I'd managed to save more money, then maybe this eviction wouldn't hit so hard. Maybe I could more easily afford a new space.

I crouched beside Bubbles, her three-legged frame warm and steady against my legs. She licked my hand as if to remind me she believed in me even if no one else did.

"We'll find something even better." I scratched her favorite spot between her shoulders. "We have to."

The weight of the situation pressed into my chest, but I refused to let it crush me.

I had less than thirty days to find a new place and make sure it could house the dogs safely. I needed time to let clients know of the location change, too. I couldn't leave that notice until the last minute because owners would need to find new accommodations if I couldn't find another home.

I kept petting Bubbles. I didn't know how I was going to pull this off, but I'd be damned if I let Mr. Pitt's greed erase everything I'd built. The center was more than a business to me.

It was my life.

One thing was for sure, I couldn't waste any time feeling sorry for myself. "First." I stood. "We'll visit Thorned Bough and get a big donation for the shelter. I'm depending on you to turn up the cuteness factor." As if she understood me, she tilted her head at an adorable angle. "Then we'll stop at the real estate office and see what's available."

I had less than thirty days to make a miracle happen, and I couldn't waste a second. "Let's go."

6

———————

My ancient Volvo station wagon looked woefully out of place at the Thorned Bough vineyard. A traditional timber-frame house that somehow managed to look modern dominated the landscape. Of course, it would have multiple decks that offered breathtaking views of the Candle River and the White Mountains. And perfect rock walls, housing perfect gardens with perfect red, orange, and yellow flowers I had no name for.

"Would you look at this place!" I said to Bubbles as I parked on the gravel driveway. "Oh, look! There's a three-season porch." One of my bucket-list items was to own a home with a three-season porch. I sighed. "Mr. Gaines has good taste."

In the back seat, Bubbles' tail brushed the vinyl.

To the right of the house lay a sweeping view of yellowing vines on trellises, glinting golden under the fall sun. I gripped the steering wheel, wishing the knots in my stomach would unravel. "Right, calm down, Lark. We need this donation. Mom said this Oliver Gaines has a good heart."

I turned off the ignition and got out, then opened the back door to let Bubbles out. She sat on the seat, anticipation shining in her eyes. The heart bandana and bright pink harness made her look happy and bright. "All right, Bubbles. Time to work your magic."

As if she understood, Bubbles let out a chipper woof and hopped out of the car, tail wagging.

I reached inside and brought out the folder I'd prepared. It held photos of dogs in need of a home to tug at his heartstrings and also event plans and financials to cater to his business side. I took in a long breath. Hopefully, I'd crafted just the right balance of heartfelt story and persuasive data.

Bubbles and I strode up the granite steps, stopping in front of the massive oak door. I'd rehearsed my pitch for this newcomer to Brighton a hundred times. "You've got this."

Holding my breath, I knocked on the door and plastered a smile on my face.

But when the door glided open smooth as silk, my smile slipped. My breath hitched. "Aimee?"

What was *she* doing here?

Everything faded—the warm light spilling from the inside, Bubbles, my goal. My vision narrowed to just Aimee, the girl who'd crushed me with one careless betrayal. Added to that, my mother's betrayal, because she'd known exactly who Oliver Gaines was and had sent me here, knowing how I felt about seeing Aimee again.

The woman clutching the oak door still had Aimee's familiar face, but nothing else about her was recognizable. Her brown hair was cut in a stylish shoulder-length bob instead of a messy ponytail. Her raspberry cashmere cardigan and black wool pants looked boutique chic rather than the second-hand shop jeans and T-shirts she used to wear. The diamond on her ring finger could support a third-world country—a far cry from the homemade jewelry we'd crafted on long, lazy summer afternoons.

"Lark?" Aimee's eyes widened and her smile brightened her

whole face. Then her smile faltered. "I didn't think—" She shook her head. "I'd hoped—" She opened the door wider. "I'm ... glad you came. Come in, please!"

My first instinct was to turn around and leave, fast. But the tug from Bubbles' leash reminded me that I couldn't just go. The dogs needed me to see this through.

"I'm here to see Oliver Gaines, Thorned Bough's new owner," I managed to say, standing stiff as a starched sheet at the threshold.

Aimee's eyes shone with pride. "That's me. Well, my husband. I'm Aimee Gaines now."

I blinked. "You?"

"My husband and I just bought Thorned Bough. We moved back to Brighton from Savannah right before harvest." Her tone was cheerful as she searched my face, looking for what I wasn't sure.

I'd heard she'd gone away to school in Georgia and got a degree in preservation design. I couldn't help wondering what she wanted to preserve. Certainly not our friendship.

"Oliver was looking for a new challenge," Aimee babbled on. "And, well, I wanted to come back home. My mom isn't getting any younger. When our offer for the vineyard was accepted, it felt like fate."

Bubbles tapped a paw against Aimee's pantleg.

"*Good girl*," Bubbles woofed.

For a second, I was afraid Aimee would push the dog away with her foot. She'd never particularly cared for dogs and hated it when I insisted on bringing along whatever stray I'd found on our adventures. Instead, she crouched down and gave Bubbles' shoulders a good scrub. "Who is this sweetie?"

"Bubbles."

Aimee looked up at me, eyes pleading. "Please, Lark. Come in. Let's talk."

Not for Aimee. For the dogs.

Reluctantly, I followed Aimee into the house. The interior screamed of money and comfort: rustic beams, a stone fireplace, large windows showcasing the river and the mountains. The scent of rich coffee mingled with the faint tang of lemon wood polish and wealth. A stark contrast to the scent of kibbles and dog feet I could never quite wash out of my clothes. Everything about this house shouted of solidity and permanence. The kind I'd probably never have, given my choice of occupation, no matter how hard I scratched and clawed.

Aimee strode to the open-concept kitchen and reached for a coffeemaker that looked as if it needed an engineering degree to work. "Coffee?"

"No, thank you. This won't take long." I set the folder on the granite counter. Aimee had always wanted the high life, and she'd found it. She moved so easily in this space. As if she truly did belong. A pang of something knocked in my chest, but I ignored it. I didn't want what Aimee had. I wanted something more than to be a trophy wife. Like Max, I had an important mission to fulfill.

Bubbles sniffed at everything in sight, tail giving a tentative wag when Aimee bent down to pat her again. I tightened the leash—an instinctive claim.

"What happened to her leg?" Aimee's hand hovered over Bubbles' head as if seeking permission to touch her. Bubbles shifted her head forward to accept the pat.

"Accident. Her owner couldn't afford the surgery, so Dr. Ava saved her. Now she's looking for a new forever home."

Bubbles nosed her head forward for another pat. "She's adorable."

"She'd be too much work for you. All that daily brushing and hair shedding. It would make a mess of your lovely couches and wood floors. Not to mention your clothes."

"Wow, you're going right there."

I ignored her comment, forcing myself to tamp down the

growing growl in my gut. I opened the file and took out the photos, lining them up on the counter. "I came to ask Mr. Gaines if he'd be willing to make a donation to the Adopt-a-Thon taking place at the Pumpkin Festival. We're looking for a silent auction prize that's big enough and fantastic enough to draw attention to the Tri-Town Dog Shelter. It's in dire need of funds to keep it going through the winter."

I added the plans and financials to the photos. "There's a rumor in town that Mr. Gaines is looking for ways to have community involvement. This would be a great start."

Aimee rose, glancing through the papers I'd spread out on the counter. "It sounds like a wonderful cause."

My hope flared, only to die down at the sight of Aimee's downcast face.

"But ..." My hands pressed into my thigh, bracing myself for the coming brush-off.

"Things are tight right now." She lifted a shoulder, let it drop. "The vineyard and the house needed a lot of urgent repairs before we could move in. The harvest wasn't great because of the neglect. And we're having to invest a lot into upgrades so that the vineyard will succeed, if not next year, then the year after."

I forced a nod, my fists clenching tighter on my thighs. "I understand."

Except that I didn't. How could Aimee, with her perfect house and her perfect life, not spare a sliver of that perfection to help dogs like Bubbles?

I'd promised myself that I wouldn't beg. I couldn't stoop that low, especially not in front of Aimee. "These dogs have nowhere else to go. They need a safe haven while they wait for new owners."

"I'll see what I can do."

"Any donation would help." The answer probably wouldn't change. "The shelter's overcrowded, and if we don't find homes for at least twelve dogs, some of the older and infirm dogs will have to be put to sleep."

Aimee's throat bobbed as her gaze snapped down to Bubbles. No way I'd let Bubbles get on the list. She had too much to give to the right owner. But I wasn't going to tell Aimee that.

"Do you still talk to dogs?" she asked.

I brushed away her comment. I would never admit that I could to the person who used my ability as a bomb to destroy my life. "*Pfft!* That was just a childhood notion. I'm a professional dog trainer now."

"Of course." She stepped to the other side of the counter and poured herself a mug of coffee. "I would like to apologize for what I did back then."

"Kinda late for that. Not that destroying my life got you what you wanted. Those girls dropped you like last-year's fashion as soon as they got what they wanted from you."

Bubbles whined at my feet, her eyes scrunched with worry. I patted her head.

"That's where you're wrong." Aimee's fingertips turned white against the sides of the mug she held firmly with both hands. "I dropped *them*. I tried to explain, but you wouldn't let me."

"You have no idea what you did to me, do you?"

"I—"

I rose from the high stool and tugged on Bubbles' leash. "Let's go." I tipped my chin toward the file. "I'll leave that with you. If you could please ask Mr. Gaines to look over the data and think about giving something, anything toward the cause."

She nodded.

I swallowed the lump in my throat. Seeing her again hurt even more than I imagined it would. "Thank you for your time."

Movements mechanical, I headed toward the front door, Bubbles hopping at my side.

"Lark, wait." Aimee placed the mug on the counter and came toward me. She stopped midway, hands knotted at her belly, looking contrite. "I ... I know things ended badly between us, but I'd like to fix that. You're part of the reason I wanted to move back to Brighton. Oliver and I are thinking of starting a family—"

"Congratulations." I couldn't quite keep the bitterness out of my voice.

"And I want my child to have the kind of childhood we had."

A rush of memories, all those golden summers running around as if we didn't have a care in the world. All the fun and laughter. Closer than sisters. Bubbles nudged my hand, her black nose cold against my palm. The weight of her silent encouragement was a lifeline pulling me back from the swirling tide of old memories and fresh disappointment. "Until her best friend breaks her heart."

"I'm trying to make things right."

I shook my head, the words tumbling out before I could stop them. "I thought you were my friend. My best friend. I trusted you with everything and you—" My voice cracked, the raw edge of my hurt slipping through. "You used me."

"I was young. Stupid. I made a terrible mistake." Aimee's eyes misted, and for a moment, she looked like the girl I used to know. "Lark, I regret—"

She took a step closer, but I held up a hand to stop her.

"No, you don't get to explain it away. You don't get to make it better now, not after all this time." My arms wanted to wrap around my middle in a feeble attempt to hold in the anger and pain so ready to spill. "You let me believe our friendship was real, then you threw it all away. Do you know what that did to me?"

"I do," she whispered, voice trembling. "I've missed you, Lark. You were my best friend. I know I can't undo the past, but I want to try to make amends."

I gave a sharp nod. "A donation would be a great start."

"Please, meet me for coffee sometime? Someplace neutral?"

For a moment I considered her offer, if only to hear what trumped-up excuses she'd find for what she did. But I didn't want to sit with her. I didn't want to hear what she had to say. I wanted to drive away from Thorned Bough and never see her again. And yet, the dogs' futures loomed larger than my old wounds. There was still a chance her husband would agree to help the dogs.

I'd gotten past the betrayal, if not the hurt. I'd made a good life for myself in spite of a lot of people still thinking of me as "that odd girl who talks to dogs." If I could use her to help the dogs, the way she'd used me to get into the "it" girls' clique at school. Then, maybe, it would wipe the slate clean.

"I'll think about it." Just not now. Not until I could put up stronger armor.

"I'll be here when you're ready," Aimee called after me.

I stepped out into the crisp autumn air, heart heavy. I'd failed. I hadn't gotten the big donation. The colorful tree leaves and golden vine leaves, swaying in the breeze, mocked my heartbreak.

I opened the car door for Bubbles. "We'll figure it out." My voice sounded splintered. "We have to."

"*Good girl?*" Bubbles woofed.

"The best. The failure was all mine." I'd let emotions get in the way of my goal.

Bubbles let out a soft woof and licked at my face while I hooked her seat belt, making me chuckle.

As the vineyard disappeared in my rearview mirror, my grip tightened on the steering wheel. The golden vines blurred in the distance, the brightness of the day dulled by the sting of my failure. Bubbles rested her head on the back of my seat, her nearness grounding me.

"*Good girl*," Bubbles woofed.

I reached back and petted her. "The best."

As I drove past the Thorned Bough sign and turned onto the main road, Aimee's words echoed in my mind: *"I'm trying to make things right."* A sharp pang twisted in my chest. Was she? Could she?

I shook my head, trying to clear the longing for something that could never be.

Ahead the winding road stretched, flanked by maples ablaze with red, orange, and gold. Somewhere out there, the solution to save the shelter waited. I didn't need Aimee or her husband or their donation. The Gaines weren't the only Brighton residents with deep pockets.

I couldn't afford to dwell on Aimee, on what we'd lost, or what could have been.

But as the wind swept through the trees, scattering a flurry of red and gold leaves, I couldn't quite shake the thought that maybe I wasn't as over her betrayal as I wanted to believe.

7

Because I was still reeling from dealing with Aimee, I decided to stop at the center and drop off Bubbles before heading to see Lara Bishop of Bishop Realty about a possible new home for the dogs. I wasn't sure I had the mental fortitude to find out that nothing out there was in my price range, but I couldn't procrastinate. I had to find a new place fast.

I arrived at the center to find utter chaos. The dogs barked, not in their usual playful way, but in mayhem of high-pitched yips, low growls, and an urgent howl from Hercules, all blending into a deafening cacophony.

Rae zipped from one dog run to another. "This isn't funny."

My fingers tightened on Bubbles' leash before I released her. She raced in her odd gait to the play area to add her voice to the noise, increasing the nagging feeling that something wasn't right. "What's not funny?"

At the door of a sleep suite, Rae froze in place, eyes wide, mouth agape. "Max," she finally squeaked out. "I can't find him anywhere."

"He couldn't have gone very far." I tried to sound calm, but my voice wavered. This couldn't be happening. Not today. Not Max.

Rae shoved her hands into her jeans pockets, raising her shoulders around her ears. Her lips trembled as if she expected a verbal lashing. "The thing is, I don't think he's inside. I've looked everywhere. Twice."

Max, what have you done? I plopped my bag and car keys on the reception counter. I scanned the chaotic play area. "Was a door left open?"

"Not as far as I know. But a whole bunch of daycare dogs came in at the same time, so it was a zoo for a bit. After everyone settled, that's when I noticed he was gone." Rae's voice broke on the last word.

I blew out a breath, trying to keep my frustration in check. Snapping at Rae wouldn't help anyone. It certainly wouldn't help locate Max. "I'm not angry, Rae. I'm just worried about Max."

"Me, too."

"Okay, let's do this strategically. You call the neighbors and ask if anyone's seen him. I'll keep looking through the building. He's little and could be hiding in a small space somewhere."

Rae nodded like a bobblehead doll. "Okay, okay. I can do that. I can make calls."

While she headed for the reception counter, I went through each room, looking into every nook and cranny, calling after Max, my voice echoing off the walls. "Max? Max!"

I figured I'd find him with the food, but he wasn't there. The equipment room was empty. His sleep suite was also empty, his favorite squeaky dragon abandoned. I couldn't sense his presence anywhere. Somehow, he'd managed to run away. But to where?

The thought of Max, as ornery as he was, wandering alone out there made my chest tighten. His small size would make him easy prey for bigger animals and make him invisible to drivers. And if animal control found him before I did ...

No, I couldn't go there. I had to find him first.

"Lark?" Rae called out to me.

"Yes?"

"Someone on the phone wants to talk to you."

"Can you handle it?" I opened the back door and checked the outdoor play area, just in case he'd wanted some fresh air. A blast of cold breeze hit me, but no sign of Max.

"No, he insists."

Probably Mr. Pitt, the landlord, looking for his rent check, even though it wasn't due until the end of the day. Did I have enough in the center's account to write that check? "Coming."

I reached for the phone and braced. "Hello, this is Lark."

"Why is your dog at my door?" Caleb's voice came through the speaker as sharp as the dogs' barks in the play area.

I tightened my fingers around the handset. "What do you mean?"

"The yappy white dog. Why is he at my door? Did you drop him off?"

"I have no idea where you live." Hand splayed over my heart, I blew out a breath. At least Max was safe. That stubborn little dog had managed to get what he wanted. Never mind the plan. "Give me your address, and I'll come pick him up."

Caleb gave me his address, each word clipped and curt as if he were spitting them out. He hung up before I could say anything more. The anger in his tone lingered in my mind. Was he more annoyed at Max or at me? Had I missed something?

Just what I didn't need right now, an angry—what was he? Not exactly a customer. Certainly not a friend. I settled on adoption prospect. I placed the handset back on the receiver.

"Max is safe." I grabbed my bag and car keys. "I'm going to go pick him up."

"Where is he?" Rae bit her lips as if she were afraid of the answer.

"All the way in Brighton."

Her eyes widened. "But that's, like, thirteen miles away!"

"He's one determined guy." I forced a weak smile. I had to admire his moxie, yet I couldn't shake the curl of dread in my gut. I hooked my bag over my shoulder and fisted the car keys in my hand. "Hold down the fort. I'll be back soon."

CALEB'S HOME turned out to be a tiny home on wheels parked on a scrap of land on the far side of Brighton Lake. The home looked not much bigger than a camper. The dark-brown siding and hunter-green shutters made it almost disappear in the sea of pines surrounding it. Only an opening that gave him a view of the lake provided relief from the fortress of trees. An orange kayak rested on a wooden tripod stand near the water. A single brown Adirondack chair faced the lake. A rock fire pit took up space between the chair and the water and looked well used. The lap of the water on the rocky shore lent a peaceful backdrop to the sound of birds and the scurry of squirrels.

The front door opened before I even had a chance to knock. Eyebrows low over his stormy eyes, Caleb pointed inside to a brown couch where Max had installed himself, twirled into a tight donut. He looked as if he had no intentions of moving. "He won't leave."

Max gave a soft woof. *"My guy."*

We talked about this, Max. This isn't the way to get what you want. "He took a shine to you when you visited the center yesterday."

Caleb's gaze flicked toward Max, just for a second, before scrutinizing me like a specimen on a slide. "You still talk to dogs?"

So, he did know who I was.

"Of course not." I brushed away his comment, feeling heat creep up my neck. "You and Liam made sure to taunt that notion right out of my head."

"Yeah, well, I'm sorry we teased you so much." He ticktocked his head. "We were kind of jealous that you could, you know, talk to them."

"You were?"

He shrugged, an I-don't-care jerk of his shoulders. "It seemed like a superpower back then, and Liam and I were both into superheroes at the time."

They'd started edging me out of the trio during their superhero stage, saying girls couldn't be superheroes, never mind that I pointed out everyone from Supergirl to Wonder Woman. Good thing Aimee had moved to town that summer. A new friend, just when I'd needed one. She'd even liked to play as hard as I did back then. *Don't think about Aimee!*

"Yeah, I remember that phase." I tried not to chuckle, but it came out like a rush of pebbles. "You guys running around town with capes and getting into all kinds of trouble."

"Not our finest summer." He chucked his chin toward Max. "Can you take him?"

"*Not leaving,*" Max woofed, tightening his donut posture. "*My guy.*"

As Caleb stared at the dog, a muscle twitched in his jaw. He crossed his arms over his chest, a stance as rigid as the walls of his tiny home.

"You're sure you don't want him to stay." I stared at Max, willing him to play cute. Right on cue, Max scooted along the couch until he reached the edge closest to Caleb's knees. Max let out an exaggerated sigh and stretched one paw to flop dramatically over his eyes.

Caleb's lips pressed tight.

"You did come to the center to get a companion. And he did help you—"

"I'm sure." The words came out like periods. Full stop. No moving him from his decision.

Still, I had to try. For Max's sake as well as Caleb's. "I've trained many dogs specifically to deal with PTSD."

Caleb sneered. "What could that thing possibly do?"

"*Hey!*" Max grumbled, lifting his head just enough to glare.

"He can sense and interrupt or alert you to your rising anxiety. He can calm and comfort you during an anxiety attack. He can block—"

"He's not big enough to block anything more than a loaf of bread."

Max snorted. "*As if.*"

"Well, if you give me a chance to train both of you, you'll see that he can. He can also cover your back. He's already a loyal friend. Look at him, he's ready to bite my hand if I try to take him away."

"*You betcha.*"

Caleb grunted, his gaze flicking back to Max. At his side, his fingers curled as if he had to work to keep himself from reaching out.

"Do you get nightmares?" I wrapped the question in as cloud-soft a tone as I could.

He blew out a breath, tensing his whole body. Max, sensing the shift, stretched out to bop Caleb's knee with his nose.

Caleb didn't move.

"He can gently wake you up from a nightmare."

"I just—" He swiped a hand through his shaggy hair. "It was suggested ... I thought I could ... But can't. I just can't be responsible for anyone right now. Not even a dog."

Which again made me wonder what had happened to him. He was obviously in distress, and a dog could make a huge difference in his quality of life, if he'd just let it.

Max shifted so he could press his head against Caleb's knee. Caleb seemed to relax the tightness of his fist.

"How about this?" I stuffed my hands in my jeans pockets, elbows splayed out. "I'll take both of you through training sessions. Maybe three a week. More if you decide you want more. I'll get Max ready to pass the Public Access Test, and help you two work together, find your cues—"

"Public Access Test? Cues?"

"Let's say you're out in a crowd and you start feeling like it's too much, you could give Max a signal that would make him, let's say, paw at your leg. Then you could use Max as an excuse to leave. You could say he needs to go to the bathroom. Nobody would call you on that."

"I don't want people to know ..."

I sighed. No, he couldn't show any signs of weakness. "You mean your brothers."

The tightening of his jaw gave me his answer. Mitchell and Ryan were both much older than Caleb and had teased their baby brother mercilessly about being weak. They were both rough and tumble football players in high school. And Caleb had no interest in team sports, preferring, like Liam, to run track instead.

"You can just say he's my dog and that we're old friends spending time together now that you're back in town. I mean, we used to hang out together all the time."

He snorted. "In grade school."

"You're still Liam's friend, and I'm Liam's sister." I lifted my shoulders and eyebrows, hoping the old connection would work. "Nobody has to know that Max is training to be your service dog."

"I don't need a service dog. Especially not one that tags me as crazy."

"Using a psychiatric service dog doesn't mean you're crazy. Far from it. It just means that he can do specific things to help you. And by law, that means he's allowed to go wherever you go. A companion, even a therapy dog, can't." I opened both my arms in a way that encompassed his tiny home in the woods, his hideout from the world, his safe space. Dishes sat in the sink, gathering dust. A stack of unopened mail took up prime counter real estate. The remnants of fried fish lingered in the air. The living room looked as if Caleb crashed here, but didn't belong. Temporary. Was that why his home had wheels?

"And I'm guessing that when you're alone here, you're mostly okay. It's being out and about that might trigger you."

Caleb swallowed hard, his inner turmoil evident in the swirling light in his eyes. Max nudged Caleb's knee again. Patient. Steady. A quiet presence in a storm.

"I don't know ..."

"Tomorrow's Saturday. How about we meet outside the dog park and just enjoy a walk by the lake together? All three of us."

His gaze held an ocean of emotions, waves roiling as if storm-tossed. He exhaled, slow and deep, as if he were forcing the decision out of his chest. He dropped his gaze. "Take him home."

Max lifted his head, his entire body taut. *"Don't make me go,"* he whined.

"Max!" *If you come now, you'll have a chance to prove you deserve to stay. Play stubborn and that's the end. Got it?* "Come!"

Max took his time stretching backward, then forward, giving us both his most bored yawn, then a snort. He hopped off the couch, shook himself, then hesitated at the door. He tipped his head to one side as if asking Caleb if he was sure.

As they stared at each other, a long beat passed.

Caleb rubbed a hand over the dark stubble on his chin, then turned away as if that could shut down whatever war waged inside him. His voice came out gruff. "Go."

Reluctantly, Max trotted to my side and sat, tail a white blur —one last bid to have Caleb change his mind.

I clipped a leash to Max's collar, but he didn't follow me right away. He watched Caleb as if he saw something even I couldn't see. "*He needs me.*"

I know. "Come on. Let's go."

The door shut behind us.

We stepped off the tiny porch, but before we reached the car, Max let out a loud whine, feet dragging.

I glanced over my shoulder.

The curtain in the front window shifted.

Max woofed, tail a metronome.

For just a moment, Caleb stood there, silhouetted by the dim light of his tiny house, watching us leave. He looked like a man trying to convince himself he didn't care.

And failing.

8

On Saturday morning, before meeting with Caleb at the dog park, I stopped by Lara Bishop's real estate office in downtown Brighton, Max in tow.

I pulled the door open, glaring down at Max. "Behave in there."

He gave me a surly look. "*Me?*"

"Yes, you."

The sound of a far-off *ding-dong* echoed and ebbed in the empty office. No one sat at any of the three desks placed artfully in the small space. Each area had its own rug, padded customer chairs, and lush plants. The muted shades of blue and gray on the walls added to the air of cool efficiency. The air smelled of rich coffee and the potted hostas strategically placed around the room.

"Hello?" I gripped Max's leash as he trotted ahead, tail wagging, stopping only at the tug on his harness. "Lara?"

"*Smells like bacon,*" he woofed, tail beating the air.

No bacon.

A crash came from the small room off the back wall. "Shoot!"

A woman came out, dark head bent forward, paper towel swiping at a coffee stain that went from the chest of her white blouse down to the waistband of her navy pencil skirt. A gesture I knew too well.

I didn't quite manage to swallow my groan. Not Aimee.

At the sound, her head snapped up. The hand dabbing at her blouse stilled.

"Oh, hi!" Her smile see-sawed with a frown as if she couldn't decide which was more appropriate.

I bit my tongue and held it there for a moment until I could modulate my voice into something that could pass for civil. "What are you doing here?"

Max parked himself next to me, nose twitching. *There's bacon.*

Shhh!

Aimee tossed the coffee-stained paper towel into the trashcan by the far desk and smoothed her skirt. "I work here." Her chin cranked up. "Not too many restoration jobs available. I got my real estate license in Georgia. When we moved here, I took the New Hampshire exam. Lara needed help, and well ..." She made a ta-da gesture. "Here I am."

I clenched the leash tighter, as if that could keep old hurts at bay. "I'm looking for Lara."

"She's, uh, out with a client."

"Okay, I'll come back." I pivoted to leave, dragging Max along.

"No, wait! I can help you."

I wasn't sure I could trust her help. "I don't think so."

"Please, Lark." She opened an arm in invitation. "At least let me take notes for Lara. It'll save you some time."

Every cell in my body wanted to say no, but time wasn't a luxury I had. I had less than three weeks to find and refurbish a center for the dogs. Or close permanently. My throat worked around the bitterness.

"Who's this cutie?" Aimee bent forward, reaching for Max's head.

"Max the Terrible."

"*Hey!*" he barked, just as I expected him to.

Aimee yanked her hand back and straightened as if she'd narrowly escaped a bite. Just as I'd wanted her to. I was not a nice person around Aimee.

"He's in training." I gave her a tight smile. "Needs a lot of work."

Max huffed, shuffling his front feet. "*As if.*"

Aimee gestured to one of the plump chairs in front of her desk. I sank in and my body sighed at the comfort. When was the last time I'd sat in that comfy a chair? I couldn't remember.

Max hopped up on the empty chair next to mine, twirled three times and flopped down into a donut. Less than a minute later, he was snoring.

A pewter frame on Aimee's desk caught my eye. A wedding photo. Of course, Oliver Gaines was magazine-model hand-some. Of course, they made the perfect couple—Aimee in her princess dress, veil cascading for miles and Oliver in a dapper morning coat and top hat. The romantic vineyard sunset behind them offered a flawless backdrop to their flawless life.

I'd expect no less from Aimee than an Instagram-worthy wedding, given the dreams we'd shared under skies of stars on hot summer nights. Getting married, having a family, that's what Aimee had dreamed of. Neither were part of my life plan.

My tongue itched to ask her about her husband's donation to the shelter. But that would have to wait. Center first. Then the shelter.

Aimee took out a Bishop Realty navy-and-gold pen, poised it over a fresh pad of paper. "So, what are you looking for?"

My dreams had woven around having the best canine center in the state, running a successful business. Admitting I wasn't flourishing cost me. "My landlord isn't renewing my lease for the canine center in Stoneley. I need to find new space before the end of the month."

"That's a tight schedule."

"Tell me something I don't know."

Her lips twitched, but she kept her tone professional. "Are you looking to buy or lease?"

"In a perfect world? Buy." And not have to worry about landlords pulling the rug out from under me. "But I don't have time to line up financing right now." I wasn't about to admit to the sad state of my finances. "So, rent."

"What's your range?"

I rattled off my meager budget. She blinked. Not a good sign.

"How many square feet do you need?"

I listed the center's needs: two indoor play areas, at least six dog runs, a grooming space, an equipment room, office, lobby and two outdoor play areas.

Aimee scribbled, nodding along with the strokes of her pen. "Is Stoneley still your ideal location?"

"Yes, but I know I can't be picky right now."

"Out in the country or in town?"

"Ideal? An easy access from Stoneley, Granite Falls and Brighton."

"Okay, I'll look for something central."

"Lara."

"Yes, of course, Lara will look. How barky are the dogs?"

"Barky?"

She lifted a brow. "Would neighbors complain about the noise?"

"Lara would already know the answer."

Aimee met my gaze. "Well, Lara isn't here. So, unless you want to wait until she has time, you're stuck with me." She poised her pen over the pad once more. "Barky?"

"Maybe."

"Space between building, then."

"I just need a place, Aimee. Fast. Something I can easily convert into a canine center."

"I'm not going to lie."

An involuntary snort came out.

Aimee ignored it. "Finding something won't be easy. The market is tight right now." She tapped her pen against the desk. "Can you run your business from home?"

"Too far out of town. And too small."

As Aimee glanced at her notes, she chewed on her bottom lip—something she used to do when she concentrated while studying. "I'll pass this information on to Lara. Maybe she can work a miracle."

I needed a miracle. And I hated having to depend on Aimee to pass on information.

Though it grated me to say it, my mom had raised me right. "Thank you."

Aimee tipped her head toward a shoulder. "I meant what I said. About helping the Adopt-a-Thon. Maybe I could design a poster for the event?"

Hope filled her voice, softening something inside me.

I shrugged, remembering the myriad sketches adorning her notebooks at school. She'd had a knack for capturing the essence of a person with her pencil. "Talk to Phoebe Flowers at the Tri-Town Shelter."

Aimee's too-wide smile wobbled. "I will."

I made a show of glancing at my ancient watch with the crazed glass, barely seeing the time beneath the cracks. "I have to go."

I got up and turned toward Max.

"Of course." She hesitated. "Lark?"

I lifted an eyebrow.

"I ... I might already have some place in mind. But if you'd rather wait for Lara ..."

That stopped me cold. Aimee had a lead?

Now I had to decide if my grudge was worth more than finding a safe place for the dogs.

I could wait until Monday. For Lara. A few days wouldn't make a difference. Then I wouldn't have to deal with Aimee.

Max snorted in his sleep. So small and vulnerable. He depended on me to keep him safe. Like Bubbles and Sadie and Hercules.

I sighed and sat back down. "Tell me about it."

Aimee's smile brightened. I saw a flicker of something real in her eyes—a bridge, waiting for me to cross.

9

———

By the time I got to the dog park, I was emotionally drained from dealing with Aimee once more, and wasn't sure I could handle dealing with Caleb. He was already there, sitting by himself on a hill in the shade of an oak tree, focused on the dogs playing in the two fenced areas. Helping him, helping Max would help drive all this Aimee roller coaster away.

Both sides of the dog park were filled with dogs, barking and racing in circles, their owners chatting in chairs by the gates. Off to one side, parents shouted encouragement to their kids from the sidelines of the soccer fields. Out on the lake a couple of sailboats leaned into the wind. The scent of hot dogs and autumn swirled around us.

Max sniffed the air and tugged at the leash. *"Hot dog!"*

Not now.

When Max saw Caleb, his ears perked and his tail wagged so hard his whole body wobbled. *"He's here! He's here!"*

He lunged forward practically yanking me off my feet.

I tightened my grip on the leash. *Slow down, Max. You don't want to scare him away.*

He huffed but obeyed. "*Right. Slow.*"

Caleb glanced over his shoulder, spotted us and stiffened. His hands curled over his bent knees and his shoulders hiked up as if bracing for impact. Max, vibrating with excitement, could barely contain himself.

I waved at Caleb. He didn't return the gesture, just stared as Max all but dragged me the last few steps.

Once there, Max sat by Caleb, then pawed at his knee.

Caleb flinched as if any contact was dangerous. "What does he want?"

"For you to pet him." I crouched down and rubbed Max on his favorite spot behind his ears. "He thinks you're his."

Max scooted closer and licked Caleb's hand.

Caleb yanked his hand away and scrubbed the dampness against the leg of his jeans. "I thought you didn't talk to dogs anymore."

"I don't have to. He's making it pretty obvious that he likes you. He was upset when you left on Thursday without him. That's why he ran away to find you yesterday."

"You said you didn't know where I lived, so how did he find me?"

I shrugged a who-knows. "Dogs have highly sensitive noses. They also have an uncanny ability to connect with their owners. There are tons of stories out there of dogs hiking hundreds, thousands of miles to reunite with their persons."

Caleb rubbed a hand over his face. "I'm not his person."

"But he thinks so." I stood, brushing dirt off my jeans. "Ready for that walk?"

His expression shuttered. "I don't see the point."

Max pawed at Caleb's leg. "*Tell him I can help him.*"

I grinned. "The whole point of this exercise is to spend time together. Two old friends catching up after years apart."

Caleb stared at Max as if he were a piece of a puzzle he didn't quite know where to fit. Then at me with the same expression, making me smile. When Caleb stood, Max's tail wagged so hard it almost knocked him over. The corner of Caleb's mouth twitched.

We strolled toward the lake, Max trotting between us, his whole body radiating with pride. I breathed through the tension swirling around Caleb, made myself relax, not wanting to break the fragile equilibrium between us.

When we reached the rocky shore, Max barked and play bowed in front of Caleb. Who could stay tense around a dog wanting to play?

Max barked. "*I'm a fun guy.*"

Caleb frowned. "What's wrong with him?"

"He wants to play." I pulled a tennis ball out of my pocket and lobbed it across the grass. I let go the leash and Max bolted after it, chugging like a locomotive, kicking up dirt. He bounded back to us and dropped the slobbery ball at Caleb's feet.

Caleb hesitated. Then, without looking at me, he picked up the ball and threw it. Hard.

Max chased it as if his life depended on it. He caught it on the fly, the force of the catch, rolling him over in the grass. When he returned, he dropped the ball right on Caleb's foot. Eyes bright, tongue lolling, he waited for another throw. "*I did good, right?*"

Aware of Caleb, of the emotions swirling through him, I wasn't quite sure what to do with my hands, so I stuffed them in my back pockets. "He's having fun."

Caleb rolled his eyes but pitched the ball again. And again. With each throw, Caleb's shoulders lost some of their rigidity.

Finally, Max flopped onto his belly, panting.

Caleb stared at Max. "He has a lot of energy for a small guy."

"He does."

"Maybe too much for an office job even if it is at a busy store."

"There's always before and after work. A walk at lunchtime. Weekends. Hiking—"

"He wouldn't last more than half an hour on a hike."

I smirked. "Don't tell him that. He'll take it as a challenge."

Max snorted. "*Challenge accepted.*"

Caleb shook his head, mumbling something under his breath.

I laughed. "You know, for someone who keeps saying he doesn't want a dog, you sure look like a guy considering it. You could take him home tonight and see how you get along."

Max hopped up. "*Yes, yes, yes!*"

Caleb's expression darkened. "No."

The word weighted the air between us. I didn't argue. I just let the silence stretch.

After a moment, he blew out a breath. "This service dog test. What's in it?"

"It shows that your dog can handle any public situation— elevators, restaurants, traffic, crowds."

He glanced at Max, who watched him as if he hung the moon. "Might be a problem."

"You both need a bit of training, that's all. He knows basic commands, so now it's just a matter of refining."

"Like what?"

"He needs to obey voice commands because during the test, you won't be allowed leash corrections, training aids or treats. So that's where we'll start, building the bond between the two of you." I offered him the leash. "Try walking him."

He hesitated. For a long beat he just stared at the red loop of nylon in my hand. Then he finally took it.

Max wagged his tail. "*My guy.*"

"Stand next to him." I took a step back, giving them space.

"When you want to start moving, just say 'Let's go.' Don't tug on the leash, just start walking."

Caleb wrapped the leash around his hand as if Max were a Great Dane about to bolt. He took a step forward, making sure Max followed. Max trotted next to him, chest puffed out, announcing, "*My guy.*"

Caleb frowned. "I can't have him barking like that all day long. It'll frighten customers."

"Then give a command to quiet down. I've been using 'Shhh.'"

Caleb tried it, his neck reddening as if he thought the whole exercise was silly. "Shhh!"

Max's ears swiveled toward Caleb. He went silent, staring up at Caleb as if he were the smartest human alive.

Caleb blinked. "Huh."

"Training."

We kept moving in silence. Max focused on Caleb. Slowly, Caleb relaxed his grip until the leash hung loose between them.

Yes! I smiled a little I-told-you-so-smile. "That was a great first session. When would you like to meet next?"

He hesitated, his gaze squinting down at Max, who still trotted beside him like a well-behaved dog. A muscle in Caleb's jaw flexed. He turned to face me. Max stopped and sat at Caleb's side.

"Let's test a hike. Rainbow Falls trail on Mount Candle. Tomorrow. Nine a.m.?" His casual tone held a don't-care tone. As if he didn't expect Max to live up to the challenge.

I nodded, keeping my expression neutral, but happy dancing inside. "Sounds good."

I reached for the leash. I caught the way Caleb's fingers curled around the leash as if reluctant to let Max go. Caleb looked down at the red nylon in his hands before handing it over. "I'll meet you at the parking lot trailhead."

Max sat at Caleb's feet, looking up at him with absolute devotion, tail sweeping lazy arcs against the grass. He didn't jump, didn't bark, didn't demand. He just waited.

Caleb stared down at the dog. His hand twitched as if he might reach down and pet him. But he caught himself and shoved both hands into his front jeans pockets instead. "See you tomorrow."

Max let out a quiet *wroo-wroo*.

Caleb stalked back toward the parking lot and his bike. But just before he reached it, he stopped and looked over his shoulder. His gaze landed on Max, then moved to me, making my heart beat just a little faster. Did he like what he saw? *Ugh, Lark. Not a good idea. You have enough problems as it is.*

Then he stuffed his helmet on his head, got on his bike and rode off.

I exhaled, smoothing a hand over Max's head. "You're making progress."

Max's tail thumped. "*Told ya.*"

I laughed and led him back toward town, already thinking about tomorrow and seeing Caleb again.

10

———

Sunday morning dawned crisp and bright, the air scented with damp earth and fallen leaves. The temperature was cool enough for a sweater, but warm enough to not need a coat. Sunlight filtered through the trees, shimmering on the red, orange and gold leaves, making the world appear to shine. It made me wish I had artistic talent to capture the joyful sight.

We got to the trailhead before Caleb. Max kept nipping at the backpack I'd made him wear to carry his own water and treats, his teeth clicking against the plastic clasps.

"Don't like."

"It's how you show Caleb that you can carry your own weight. You need to keep pace with us today."

Max grumbled and stopped trying to get the backpack off. He stared at the road, ears perked, tail twirling like a wound spring. Then suddenly, he stood and barked. *"He's here! He's here!"*

Sure enough, Caleb—gray reflective jacket, gloves and helmet—sped around the bend on his bicycle. As he pedaled into the parking lot, his gaze went straight to Max, and though his face remained neutral, something in his shoulders loosened.

At the edge of the parking lot, he dismounted. He smelled like clean soap and cedar as he approached, bike chain ticking with each step. My fingers tightened around the leash at the unexpected jump of my pulse. *No*, I told myself. *He's Liam's best friend. He's like a second brother.*

He headed for the trailhead sign where he locked his bike and helmet on one of the supports.

"You rode all this way?" Just as he'd biked to the canine center on that stormy day.

He stuffed his jacket and gloves into his backpack, then re-shouldered it. "Beautiful day for a ride."

"That it is." I extended Max's leash toward him. "Here."

He hesitated before taking it, his fingers brushing mine, warm and solid, for a fraction of a second longer than necessary.

"*Let's go*," Max barked, tail a blur behind him.

"He seems eager enough." Caleb shifted the leash from one hand to another, lowering sunglasses over his eyes.

I grinned. Was he trying to hide the fact that he enjoyed having Max here?

Just as we hit the trail, an ambulance siren screamed by on Mountain Road. Caleb's body went rigid. His breath hitched, sharp and shallow. His hands clenched into fists. His gaze darted, scanning as if for threats. A muscle in his jaw twitched. Then, as if realizing he needed to mask his reaction, he crouched down, pretending to relace his hiking boots. His fingers shook, knuckles whitening as he tightened the lace hard enough to cut off circulation. Sweat beaded alongside his hairline.

Max whined and tried to climb onto Caleb's lap, pressing his warm weight against Caleb and licking at his face.

"Hey, I can't lace my boots with you doing that." His tone

was both curt and softer than I expected. I noted something else, too—relief.

His hand landed on Max's back, fingers digging into the white hair, grounding himself for a second before he rose again.

I pretended to rummage through my pack for my water bottle, giving them a moment. When I turned back, the neutral mask was back on Caleb's face and his breath back to normal. His eyes were unreadable through the mirrored lenses of his sunglasses. "Ready?"

I gestured toward the trail. "You lead."

Max barked. "*I help him.*"

Yes, you do.

Caleb grabbed one of the walking sticks people left behind and hiked up the trail, Max trotting beside him. We followed the trail in silence until we reached a clearing that offered a panoramic view of Stoneley below. Sunlight dappled the town, making it look magical, like something out of a Hallmark movie. Smoke curled from chimneys, the hum of a busy weekend morning just out of reach.

"Need some water?" Caleb asked Max, pulling a water bottle from the side pocket of his backpack.

"He's carrying his own water and bowl." I lowered my pack to the ground and took a seat on a sun-warmed boulder.

Caleb tipped his head, as if seeing Max in a new light. "Good dog."

Max basked at the compliment, tail making a fast arc on the ground. He snuggled closer to Caleb's leg.

Caleb crouched and unzipped one of the pockets on Max's doggie backpack. He poured some water into Max's bowl and Max lapped it up. After putting the water bottle away, Caleb pulled out a bag of miniature treats. He shook it. "Look what I found."

Max immediately went into a sit-pretty, batting his front paws.

Caleb chuckled—an honest, warm sound that made me catch my breath. As if remembering that laughing was forbidden, he stopped and straightened. "So, you're a mooch."

"Definitely food motivated." I twirled my water bottle between my hands, debating. Did I dare bring up the subject? For Mom's sake ... "Hey, do you ever hear from Liam?"

"Sometimes." He sat on the boulder next to mine and offered Max a treat. Max gobbled it down, then pawed at Caleb's knee for another one. Caleb stared at Stoneley below, his hand resting on Max's back. "We text once in a while."

Progress, this was progress.

"How's he doing?"

"Better, I think." Caleb lobbed a treat high. Max followed the arc and nabbed it mid-air. Caleb cracked the start of a smile. "He met someone."

"Oh." That was good, wasn't it? I nodded and rolled my lips inward. "Why doesn't he call Mom?"

"Because he's ashamed." Caleb tossed Max another treat, but this time Max ignored it and pressed his head against Caleb's knee.

I took a quick sip of water and nearly choked on it. "Of what?"

"War isn't pretty."

I chewed the inside of my cheek. "Mom worries. She doesn't even know where he is for sure. Last she heard it was Germany."

"Still there." Caleb pulled out a bag of mixed nuts and offered me some. "He just can't deal with her asking him to come home. Not yet."

"Still." I took a small handful of nuts. "She—we—just want to know he's safe."

"He's safe."

The wind shifted, carrying the scent of pine and distant chimney smoke. The cold nipped at my cheeks. I missed Liam. Even when he was a pain, he was still my twin.

The silence stretched between us, thick with unspoken words.

"He's not in danger of harming himself?" The question squeaked out of my dry throat.

"I don't think so. He's looking for answers, for a way to make what he's gone through have meaning, you know?"

I didn't. Not really. Why not come home to people who loved him? I pulled out a sandwich and offered Caleb half. "Why doesn't he text me, then?"

Caleb chewed on the peanut butter-and-strawberry jelly sandwich. "Haven't had one of these in years."

"You didn't answer my question."

Caleb stuffed the rest of the sandwich half in his mouth and chewed for a long time. "He doesn't want to dim your sunshine."

"My sunshine dimmed a long time ago." Pretending, keeping up appearances was tough. To the outside world, I might look like I didn't have a care, but all my cares were eating me up inside. I guess I could understand Liam's point of view. He didn't want to have to pretend and that was easier to do around people who didn't love you. I'd had to leave Brighton to find a small measure of peace.

Caleb tossed back a handful of nuts. "I heard Aimee was back in town."

My jaw tightened. "I don't want to talk about her."

"I know she hurt you."

I nodded and bit into a chocolate bar. I didn't offer Caleb any. "Some things you can't ever forget."

"I get that."

Was that why he'd run away to the other side of the country after high school? I wanted to ask him what happened in

Seattle last spring, but he and Max were getting along so well that I didn't want to disrupt the fragile equilibrium. Instead I jumped up and tossed out a dare—something we used to do ask kids, goading each other into doing things we shouldn't. "Last one at the top buys ice cream."

This time, Caleb's half smile lit up his eyes, reminding me of the boy who'd spent almost as much time at our house as Liam. "Want to make it more interesting?"

Also something we used to do. "Like how?"

"If you lose, you make me dinner. I haven't had a home-cooked meal in forever."

"I find that hard to believe. Your mom probably cooks for you every night."

"Not every night."

"Food is how she shows her love."

"And triggers guilt."

I laughed. I got that. "I'm not sure boxed mac 'n cheese—the extent of my culinary skills—fits the bill."

He nodded, pensive. "Steaks on the grill at my house."

I wasn't sure what to make of the invitation, except that maybe I wanted to lose.

"And if I win?" I waggled an eyebrow at him, my best imitation of a villain in a black-and-white movie. "You take a selfie of you and Max and post it on the store's social media accounts."

"Deal." This time, his smile was big and real, and I wanted to hang on to it longer.

He didn't wait for me to shoulder my backpack, but sprinted up the trail, putting on his backpack on the fly. Max raced ahead, his leash dragging on the ground.

"Hey, wait up, Bud!" Caleb called.

Tail wagging, Max stopped and waited for Caleb. Then both of them flew up the side of the mountain.

I smiled. Paying for ice cream was a small price to see them bonding.

· · ·

BACK IN BRIGHTON at Sooper Scoop, Caleb licked a large coffee-toffee sugar cone, Max enjoyed a pup cup of whipped cream next to Caleb, and me a bowl of death-by-chocolate ice cream. Caleb surreptitiously patted Max's back.

Slowly but surely, we'd get there.

"Tuesday," I said, scraping up the last of my ice cream.

He licked the melting ice cream from the side of his hand. "What about it?"

"What time do you leave work?"

"Around six."

"Max and I will meet you at the store at six." We could do some training there for the Public Access Test.

I got up. "Max, come!"

Licking the whipped cream off his beard, he gave me the side-eye. "*Wanna stay.*"

Show how obedient you are.

Max snorted and trotted to me.

"What for?" Caleb wiped the stickiness off his hand with a napkin.

I gave him my brightest smile. "You'll see."

11

———

Although Aimee had offered to drive me to the property she had in mind for the new canine center, I told her I'd meet her there. Bad enough that Lara had informed me on Monday that if I wanted a new space, I'd have to work with Aimee because Lara was working on a big deal and didn't have the time, and her other agent was out on maternity leave. So, on Tuesday, I put on the thickest armor I could find—not that a sweater would protect me from more hurt—and drove to a place outside of Brighton Village, but not quite into Granite Falls.

Aimee was already there, waiting for me beside her freshly detailed black Lexus crossover SUV. Made my muddy Volvo look decrepit. She looked professional with her jacket, skirt and high heels. Next to her, I looked like a country bumpkin with my thick sweater and jeans.

Doesn't matter, Lark. Use her just like she used you.

I didn't have a dog with me and my fingers itched to run through Max's wiry hair or Bubbles' soft hair to give me courage. I shook my head and shoved open the car door. "Tear off the Band-Aid."

I greeted Aimee with a nod, keeping my distance. I stayed near my car, arms crossed, forcing her to come to me.

"Hi, Lark!" Her smile remained in place as she wisely chose to get right down to business. "I know it doesn't look like much, but—"

"It looks like it's about to fall apart." I didn't know much about architecture, but I was pretty sure roofs weren't supposed to sag that way.

"It's slated for demolition—"

"How does that help me?"

"It gives you time to look for a better place. You said you had to vacate your current space before the 31st."

I shook my head. "The slat fencing won't work. The dogs'll slip through that too easily. I can't see spending money on fencing that will get plowed over."

Aimee took a step closer, and I moved a step away. Her arms tightened around her leather portfolio. "Let's just go inside, and you'll see what I mean."

She entered a number in the lockbox and stepped inside first as if I needed leading. I lingered in the doorway, debating whether or not to follow. I closed my eyes and took in a long breath.

For the dogs.

The building smelled of dust and stale air. Not promising. Yet, under the neglect, I could make out the scent of old crayons and spilled apple juice. My gaze swept the reception area. The door on the right read, "Office" and the door on the left, "Kitchen." "What is this place?"

Aimee stepped through a door that led to a hallway, then held it open for me. "It was a daycare, so the area through here is divided into four classrooms that you could easily convert into the two play areas you wanted, a training room and add runs to the fourth."

She let me peek into each of the classrooms. They were

more closed-in than the play areas at the center, but they would do. The last classroom opened close to the back door, making it easy to let out boarders for their business—if the fencing held.

"What do you think?" Aimee asked, her face way too eager for me to love the place.

"I'd have to spend a lot of money making the conversion only to have to do it all over again after the house is demolished." I looked up at the roof. "I'm not sure the roof would hold up to snow."

A draft swept through the hallway, stirring up dust, making me shiver. Something rattled above us. Mice in the attic? Then a chunk of plaster cracked loose from the ceiling and hit the floor with a dull thud.

I raised my eyebrows. "That supposed to happen?"

Like a perfect hostess, Aimee's smile never wavered. "It's not ideal, but the structure itself is solid. The owner is willing to give you a good price, lower than what you're paying now ..."

Could it be as easy as that? Convert this space in the next two weeks, then have a few months to look for something more permanent?

"Aaron could help you," Aimee said, trying to be helpful.

Aaron would help if I asked him, but I'd already asked a lot of him with the build for the Adopt-a-Thon. He had his own life to lead; he couldn't spend it rescuing me. "Aaron has a family to support. And with the Pumpkin Festival, he doesn't have the time."

Aimee tipped her head, narrowing her gaze. "You don't have to like me, Lark. You just have to like the building."

I met her gaze for a moment before tossing back a sentence she'd used on me in high school. "Don't be so sensitive. Not everything's about you."

I strode back to the reception area, feeling Aimee's gaze following my every move. I took in the office space. Much bigger than my current office. So was the kitchen area, even though it didn't have a tub to wash the dogs. Which wasn't a deal killer; it just made cleaning up messes easier.

A scraping sound came from the front door. I turned to find a short woman with salt-and-pepper hair and a no-nonsense look coming through the door. She glanced at me, then Aimee. "Sorry, am I interrupting?"

Aimee's shoulder stiffened, but her smile stayed in place. "Not at all. We're just finishing up."

The woman nodded. "I was coming to see this space to use as a temporary storage for my business while we're doing renovation. Much cheaper than a storage locker or three."

Something in my stomach sank. I wasn't the only one eyeing this property. As much as I wanted to make things difficult for Aimee, I really couldn't lose this place. "I'm so sorry. You're too late. Aimee's already sending me the lease to review."

Aimee pressed a button on her tablet. "Done."

"Oh, well, thanks." The woman's jowls sagged and she backed out, closing the door behind her.

The phone in my pocket dinged, alerting me to a new message. I opened the door to leave.

"Lark—"

"What?" My tone was much too brusque, and I tried to rein in the roil in my gut.

Her smile finally slipped, and she shook her head. "Still punishing me, huh?"

I had no good comeback for that, so I walked out the door. But even though *she* was the one who'd betrayed me, I somehow wound up feeling like a villain in my own story.

I'D BARELY REACHED the main road when my phone rang. This old car didn't connect to my phone, so I simply reached over to the passenger seat, punched the answer button and the speaker button. "This is Lark, how can I help you?"

"Hey, Lark, it's Maeve." My cousin never called unless she needed something. "You sound like you're driving. Where are you?"

"At the old daycare on Thistle Hill off Quarry Road."

"What are you doing there?"

"Looking for a miracle."

"Sounds like there's a story there."

"I'm surprised you haven't heard it already." Given how these small towns thrived on gossip.

"Yes, well ..." She giggled, the same light, carefree sound I remembered from our childhood family Sunday dinners. A sound I hadn't heard often in the past few years. "I've been busy."

Busy getting married. Busy honeymooning in Paris. Busy moving into a storybook cottage by Brighton Lake with her baseball star husband and adorable girl. And busy turning her latest Best Bakery in New Hampshire win into even more success. I ground my teeth. "How's married life?"

"So much better than I ever dreamed."

I was happy for her. Really, I was. After all she'd gone through, she deserved her happy-ever-after. Luke loved her just as she was, and that was special indeed.

But special didn't pay the rent. And right now, that was my number one concern—finding a new home for the canine center.

"Heading to Brighton by any chance?" Maeve asked, hesitation in her voice.

I'd planned on heading to the center but turned toward Brighton instead. "Why?"

"For one thing, I have your mother's cookie order for her book club tonight."

I sighed. Going to Mom's would take me out of my way, but

I owed her for all the meals she'd brought me at the center. "For another?"

"I, uh, have a favor to ask."

Of course. I braced myself. "What kind of favor?"

"Any way you could watch Neve on Wednesday? I forgot there was a teacher workshop day. Mom's out of town. Zoe has classes. And I can't have my darling daughter here because she eats all the chocolate."

"You do realize that tomorrow is Wednesday, right?"

"I wouldn't ask if I wasn't desperate."

I should say no. I had enough on my plate right now between the Adopt-a-Thon, the center and finding Max a permanent home. Taking care of an active ten-year-old would make everything harder. But *of course,* Maeve had a last-minute problem, and *of course* she assumed I'd help.

"She'll be great company while I set up the booth at the fairgrounds," I said, more to convince myself than anything. I blame my mother for this. I grew up hearing that if I was nice, people would like me. They didn't. And yet, I still kept trying. "Speaking of chocolate, what kind of brownies are you baking today?"

"What kind do you want?"

I could go for salted caramel blondies, but I didn't want to make her win too easy for my cousin. "The fancy chocolate-raspberry ones you made last Valentine's."

"They'll be in the oven by the time you get here." Maeve let out a long breath. "Thanks, Lark. I knew I could count on you."

The line went dead.

A grumble formed low in my belly. *Of course she did.*

I exhaled, letting out all the resentment that seemed stored in my body. I glanced at my to-do list on the passenger seat—a sea of endless tasks that wouldn't do themselves.

If only all my problems could be solved with a batch of brownies.

THE BAKERY SMELLED of sugar and spice and everything nice, reminding me all I'd had to eat today was a cup of coffee on my way out the door to meet Aimee. As I stood in the long line waiting for service, I focused on the menu, trying to decide what else I could get out of Maeve. My stomach twisted—not just from hunger, but from something else, too. Something I couldn't quite decipher.

My shoulders sagged as if they carried a block of concrete. A weight I was tired of carrying. The murmuring voices and the laughter from the tables, the clatter of the register tallying sales rang in my ears, too loud, too sharp.

"Lark?"

I spun toward the voice. "Oh, hi, Mrs. Singer."

Caleb's mom seemed to have aged a decade since the last time I'd seen her. Bags puffed under her eyes. Her hair had turned almost completely gray. And a new roadmap of lines creased the corners of her eyes, eyes that had a dull sheen rather than their usual bright spark. "I was hoping to run into you."

"Oh." The line moved forward one.

"You know Caleb's back in town?"

I nodded. "He came to the Canine Center looking for a dog."

"He did?" Hope sprang in her eyes. "That's excellent. Did he find one?"

"He did, but then he refused to take him home." The line moved again. The distance between me and the counter was closing, but I wasn't sure I wanted the sugar comfort waiting there anymore.

Mrs. Singer sighed. "That sounds about right. He shuts himself in the office all day, then in his tiny home all night. I'm worried about him."

I didn't want to tell her that I was, too, because that would imply we had a much closer relationship than we did. We were old friends, that was all.

"Could you …" She hesitated, twirling the thin strap of her red cross-body bag around her fingers. "Check on him once in a while?" Her smile looked forced. "A friend won't seem as intrusive as his worried mother."

My first instinct was to say no. To tell her my to-do list was already a mile long. That Caleb's problems weren't mine to fix. But the words didn't come. Instead, I swallowed hard, feeling the old familiar tug of obligation. He was an old friend. He was Liam's best friend. I couldn't help Liam, but maybe … I could help him.

The last thing I needed was to add Caleb to my to-do list.

"I can try." Not a yes. Not really. But I could already sense her expectation settling on my shoulders, pressing, pressing, pressing. "I'm not sure he's going to welcome my intrusion either."

She stared at the floor and nodded a slow, sad dip. "I understand."

And yet, I did need to get him to bond with Max and soon. Two stones—I could attempt to check on his welfare while I got them ready for the Public Access Test. So I made a quick mental adjustment for my training plans for tonight.

I rolled my lips inward. "What happened to him?"

Tears pooled in her eyes. "He was in a bad accident last March. When he came home in April, he just wasn't the same Caleb." She shook her head as if the change in her son didn't make sense. "He was always my bright boy, so full of life. So sensitive. And now…"

"You realize he has PTSD, right?"

She licked her dry lips, lips that usually were adorned with lipstick as red as her purse. "Not that he's mentioned it, but yes, it's obvious to anyone who knows him."

"Why does he ride a bike everywhere?"

Before Mrs. Singer could answer, Maeve's voice cut through the air. "Lark!"

When I turned toward Maeve, she waved me ahead of the line. "I have Aunt Kate's cookies." With a flourish she added one of her signature blue boxes on top of Mom's. "And your brownies. They're still hot, so be careful."

Maeve wiped the counter with a rag, gaze studying the surface, voice light. Too light. "What time are you planning on coming to Brighton tomorrow?"

I tensed, already sensing where this was going. "I have to check in at the Canine Center first. Make sure my helpers turned up. If all's well, I should head this way around nine."

"Perfect! Neve is so excited. She loves spending time with you and the dogs. And since you're going to the fairgrounds ... will you pick her up here?"

No sat on the tip of my tongue but wouldn't roll out. It pressed against my teeth, a quiet rebellion itching to break free. Maeve's smile had a confident ease that made everything seem like a simple request rather than another demand. How did she do that? And why did I feel so guilty for wanting to say no?

"Of course," I heard myself say. *Why do you always do that?* "That'll cost you a cheddar scone and a coffee." I hoped the request sounded like playful bartering rather than an attempt to feel as if I wasn't just giving in.

Maeve smiled a winner's smile, wide and dazzling. What did that feel like? I was so tired of being on the losing end of any stick. And really sick of feeling sorry for myself. Something had to change soon, right?

On my way out with my two bakery boxes, the bag of scones and a large coffee, Mrs. Singer stopped me with a hand on my upper arm. Even through my sweater, my skin prickled beneath her clawing fingers. "I feel better knowing you'll check in on Caleb."

I almost corrected her, almost reminded her I hadn't promised anything. But I didn't. Maybe because her pain was so obvious. Maybe because I knew that, deep down, I would do it anyway. "Of course."

But as I stepped outside into the crisp afternoon air, the weight on my shoulders didn't lift. It only settled deeper. This wasn't just about Caleb or Maeve or anyone else.

This was about me. I was done letting everyone dictate how I spent my time and energy.

I was done being walked on.

12

———

Of course, that promise to myself only lasted as far as the grocery store where I picked up steaks, Idaho potatoes and salad fixings to make the homemade dinner I'd promised Caleb last Saturday if I lost the race to the top of the mountain. At least with Maeve's brownies I had a decadent dessert to offer him.

At the Canine Center, I checked on my staff. Kari, my night helper, was there, playing with the two overnight boarders and Bubbles, a biology textbook spread out in front of her. Hercules chilled on a pillow by the wall. Max was busy making his favorite dragon stuffy squeak before tossing it in the air, catching it and shaking it all around. The golden, the shepherd and Bubbles took turns at dropping tennis balls in Kari's lap. She pitched them and the dogs raced to go retrieve them.

"Goodnight, Kari. I'm taking Max with me." I opened the play area door and called Max over. Dragon still clutched in his jaw, he grumbled.

We're going to go see Caleb.

"*My guy.*" Tail high, Max dropped the dragon and trotted to the front door.

"I already gave Hercules his joint meds," I called to Kari. "The dogs will need feeding by seven."

"Feed at seven. Got it!" She waved at me over her head, gaze still on her biology book. I envied her multi-tasking ability.

I stopped the car in front of the Country Store. Caleb lounged near the big front window, displaying rakes and leaf blowers, looking like a manly mannequin designed to entice sales.

Tail beating madly, Max popped his front paws on the car door and barked out the window. *"I'm here!"*

Caleb shook his head and pushed himself off the brick wall. As he neared, I cranked the window down. "Get in!"

"In, ya!" Max barked.

Caleb rested an arm on the roof and peered down at me. "Where are we going?"

I pointed toward the grocery bag in the footwell. "Home-made dinner on your grill with some training while the potatoes bake."

A ghost of a smile played on his lips. And that wasn't good, because it kicked me in the chest and sparked ideas I shouldn't have. This was *Caleb*.

"I'll meet you there." He pushed off the car. "I rode my bike."

I could no longer see his face, so I leaned across the seat. "You can put it in the back. There's room."

He tapped the roof once with a hand. "I'll meet you there."

"But it's dark!"

"I've got a light." The words were like a moat: do not cross. Without waiting for a reply, he jogged away toward the back of the store. If I wasn't careful, he'd lift the drawbridge and Max and I would have no access.

"Car accident." I put the car in gear. That had to be why he rode his bike everywhere, the cause of his PTSD. What had happened to traumatize him so much? "That's going to make training even harder."

Max woofed. "*I smell bacon.*"

"You always smell bacon." I took the opportunity to fill the car with gas, watching my bank account drain with each click of the meter. I really hoped that temporary home worked out. I wasn't sure yet how I'd pay to convert one of the rooms to dog suites, but I'd find a way; I always did. What if I could make the suites portable and use them in whatever space I found next? Then it would seem less like wasted money. Something to consider.

Then I drove like a turtle to Caleb's house, giving him plenty of time to pedal there ahead of us. Somehow, we all arrived at the same time. Caleb dismounted his bike and leaned it against his tiny home on wheels. Without a glance our way, he disappeared into his house, leaving us stranded outside. I couldn't decide if I should knock on the door or walk right in. He came back out, minus his reflective cycling gear and with a bucket of kindling, wearing a hunter-green sweater that hugged him nicely and made my stomach quiver.

"Steaks, right?" he said.

"That's what you asked for." I cranked on a smile and lifted the grocery bag. "I'll need access to your oven for the potatoes."

"Let's make campfire potatoes. So much tastier."

"*I like tasty.*" Max lunged toward Caleb. I called him back and unhooked the leash. He boomeranged back to Caleb, jumping up at him. "Don't reward him with attention for jumping on you. Wait until he has all four feet on the ground." I frowned at Max. "You'll have to earn your dinner, young man."

Caleb glanced down at Max. "Me or him?"

"Both."

Caleb let out a gruff chuckle, then headed toward the firepit, Max tailing him the whole way, and set out to start a fire. Down on one knee as if proposing, he worked efficiently as if he'd started fires a time or two. Even Max sticking his curious nose into everything didn't seem to bother him. He had an ease here that reminded me of the boy I knew, an ease he didn't have in town. I was glad I'd changed my plans. In no time, kindling and logs transformed into a crackling fire, his eyes unreadable in the shadows of the bright orange and yellow flames.

Satisfied with the fire, Caleb rose. "We'll let that die down to embers, then stick the potatoes in them."

He jerked a chin toward the house. "Let's go give them a jacket."

Inside the tiny space, he brought out butter, salt and aluminum foil. After I scrubbed the potatoes, he slathered one spud with butter and rolled it in salt. While I folded the first potato in foil, he slathered and salted the next.

In the small space, we bumped shoulders, hips and the occasional elbow. Each accidental touch sparked my skin even through my clothes as if I'd touched a bug zapper. I shifted aside, busying myself with putting away the foil. Noticing my retreat, Caleb frowned, then continued as if nothing had happened.

Max sat on the couch, watching every move in case something should fall off the counter to feed his insatiable hunger.

I kept stealing glances at Caleb. Every time he got close, I couldn't help but inhale his scent of soap and cedar. So much nicer than the stinky boy sweat of years past. When had Liam's best friend gotten so hot?

"How long for coals?" I asked, moving out of the tiny kitchen to catch some breathing space.

"At least half an hour." He washed the butter off his hands and wiped them on a towel.

"Great. That gives us enough time for some training."

I clipped on Max's leash, and we all trooped outside.

I handed Caleb the leash, making sure to leave plenty of space between us. "Let's see you two walk down to the fire pit."

He glanced at the leash handle as if he wasn't sure what to do with it, then looped his fingers tight around the nylon. "I've been walking since I was one. And I walked him up Mount Candle."

"He's not always obedient, especially if there's food around. He needs to respond to voice commands, not just do as he pleases."

"*Hey!*" Max bounced, dancing all around Caleb's feet, then planted himself at Caleb's side. "*I'm good.*"

Caleb said, "Let's go."

Max trotted ahead, pulling the leash taut.

Caleb groused, letting the small dog pull him along. "He's a sled dog now?"

"Don't yank back. Try stopping or turning. He'll have to stop and look at you. You could use 'stay with me' as a command."

Caleb sighed but did as I suggested. Max skidded to a halt, turned, and trotted back to Caleb's side.

"See?" I smiled. "He's learning what you want."

Caleb glanced down at Max, something shifting in expression. He let out a long breath and ruffled Max's ears. If dogs could preen, Max did.

The flames had died down and coals were already starting to form. With the neighbors hidden by trees, it looked as if we were alone in the world. Stars bloomed on the deepening sky, their reflections dancing on the lake's surface. A comforting cocoon. No wonder Caleb spent so much time by his firepit.

"Sit in the chair." I held up a treat bag. "You'll need this."

"*Bacon!*"

"Bacon is Max's favorite treat. We call that a high-value treat. He'll do anything for bacon."

As if to prove my point, Max licked his beard and focused intently on Caleb's hands, pawing at Caleb's knee for immediate gratification. "*Bacon.*"

Caleb sat in the chair and Max faced him, attention on the bag of bacon bits as if they were crown jewels and he were a jeweler.

Elbows propped on the chair's arms, Caleb stiffened. "So why did you ask to meet at the store if you wanted to make dinner?"

"I was originally going to do some training in the store. It's part of the Public Access Test, but then ..." *I met your mother at the bakery* ... Caleb was *not* a dog in need of rescuing, I reminded myself. But a man in need of comfort. Comfort that Max could provide, given a chance. "I thought of something else."

"Oh, yeah?"

"One of the things a psychiatric service dog can do is deep pressure therapy."

A muscle flinched in his jaw as if I'd reminded him he was broken. But curiosity won out. "What's that?"

"You can teach Max a signal that makes him rest his chin on your knee or lie across your body. The pressure can engage the sympathetic nervous system and calm down anxiety."

He snorted. "A whole fifteen pounds of pressure?"

"*Hey!*"

"Don't knock it till you try it."

I didn't remind him he'd already had a taste of it when Max put his head on his knee or pressed up against his side. Now, we needed to get to a point where Max performed on cue.

Caleb shrugged a shoulder. "We've gotta wait for the coals anyway."

"It's such a hardship to train with us?" I made a joke of the question, but couldn't help thinking back to high school when no one had wanted to hang out with me because of the dogs. I shook the thought away. Water under the bridge and all that. Except that, of course, I couldn't quite find a way to let it all go.

He gave me a hooded look that jammed the air in my throat. "Hardly."

Focus on the job. "Because your legs are so long and he's so short, stretch out one leg." He did. "Let me show you."

I took a couple of bacon bits from the bag, then sat on the ground, facing him, knees bent. "You want to lure him toward your knee like so, say 'yes' and reward him with the treat as soon as he places his chin anywhere near it."

Max had no problem following the bacon bit to my knee and placing his chin there to grab the treat. "Yes!"

I showed him a couple more times. "Your turn."

Caleb was as focused on the task as Max was on the bacon. As he worked with Max, as Max responded, Caleb's whole demeanor softened.

"Now that he's got it, wait a beat before giving him the bacon and reward him if he keeps his chin on your knee."

Caleb lured Max into position, then hesitated before rewarding Max. Max's chin stayed in place. Caleb's lips twitched.

With each success, Caleb's whole body relaxed.

I'd had an unrequited crush on Caleb as a teenager, but it had died when he and Liam joined the mean girls in ostracizing me for my ability to talk to dogs. He hadn't betrayed me like Aimee had, but his and Liam's teasing had still hurt. I thought he'd been my friend. And suddenly, I needed to get away from the memories before they swamped me. "You practice. Looks like the coals are ready. I'll get the potatoes."

He nodded, offering Max another bit of bacon.

"He's paying attention to you now," I said before I headed toward the house, "focusing on your every move."

Caleb ran a hand over his bristly jaw, making a rasping noise. "Feels like a ball and chain."

I laughed at the image of Max as a ball and his leash as a chain. Shaking my head, I headed back to the house and retrieved the potatoes. Following Caleb's directions, I buried the foiled spuds in the coals and returned once more to the house.

From the big picture window, I could make out Max leaning his chin on Caleb's knee for longer and longer periods of time, and Caleb relaxing more with each touch.

I turned away from the scene and set about chopping vegetables for the salad, forcing myself to ignore the ache curling under my ribs. If I wasn't careful, I'd start liking him again. And that was dangerous.

By the time I'd put the salad together, Max had hopped into Caleb's lap and both were asleep. My heart melted like chocolate on a s'more at the sight—the slow rise and fall of Caleb's chest, the way Max nestled in his lap as if he belonged there—leaving me feeling both lonely and unsettled. Never a good combination.

I reached out, fingertips grazing the cool glass of the window. Then I yanked my hand away and curled my fingers into a fist.

This was good. This was exactly what I'd wanted—for Max to bond with Caleb, for Caleb to realize he needed Max.

So why did it feel as if I was the one losing something?

I spun away from the window and wiped invisible crumbs from the counter. I needed to focus, to remind myself of the plan.

Max belonged with Caleb.

I didn't.

But as I grabbed the plate of seasoned steaks and forced myself to keep moving, to pretend none of this affected me, I couldn't shake the thought that I wanted to belong there, too.

13

Over the course of the summer, the tents that usually housed vendors at Candlewick Park for the monthly festivals were replaced with permanent wooden booths. They still smelled of sawn wood and new paint. I glanced down at my phone.

"We're at booth number 3."

Neve, dressed in purple tights, a purple fleece jacket and a neon-green skirt, looked up from her careful attention to Bubbles and scanned the booth numbers. "Over there!"

"Good eye."

The booth faced the main drag with a smaller photo booth, off to the left, complete with hay bales and pumpkins. People could take selfies there with their dogs. Behind the structure, Aaron had constructed three rings. I wished they were in a more visible spot and faced the main drag, but I got that they would impede traffic. Beyond the three rings lay a field where the dogs could go do their business. He'd even installed a potty bag stand and bin to dispose of the bags. The space was large enough to do some dog demonstrations, so the location was actually perfect.

Neve trotted ahead, Bubbles hopping at her side. She stopped at the photo booth and enticed three-legged Bubbles to leap onto a hay bale, releasing a puff of grassy air. That dog hadn't let her handicap stop her from trying anything. I wished people could see that about her.

Neve sat next to Bubbles, leaning her head against the dog's, her dark eyes wide with eagerness. "Can we try it out?"

"Of course." I lifted my phone and snapped a couple of photos.

"Lemme see." Neve grabbed my phone. "I like that one best."

"You and Bubbles look awfully cute. Maybe you can convince your mom that you need Bubbles at the cottage." I smiled, Cheshire-cat style. Maeve would love me for that suggestion.

Neve nodded and pointed at the photo. "Send it to her."

"Done." I stood staring at the door of the booth. This display had to entice enough people to stop and look at the dogs, to play with them … to take one home. Nothing was cuter than a girl with a dog. "Can I use this photo on the Adopt-a-Thon website?"

Her smile overtook her face and she nodded as if her head were on a spring. "Yes!"

I sent Maeve a quick text asking her permission to post and stating I had Neve's.

I opened the booth door to a stir of sawdust that made me sneeze. "Let's get things organized inside so I'll be able to display all the dog equipment."

"Grandma made the cutest bandana for Snick. It has jack o' lanterns and dog ghosts all over it."

"That does sound cute." Auntie Grace had gone from hating me for giving her Snickerdoodle to not knowing how she'd ever lived without the mini-labradoodle. One of my successes. Maybe I was losing my touch, though, because lately, I seemed to strike out more than hit home runs. That brought up an image of Caleb and Max sleeping together on that Adirondack chair. Too early to make a call on that one yet.

Neve peered across the center walkway. "Why is that lady staring at you?"

I turned to find Aimee in her perfect navy slacks and jacket and impractical pumps frozen in imitation of a statue at a booth cattycorner to mine. Her mouth twisted off to one side as if she were debating something, setting my nerves on edge. "I have no idea."

I turned my back to her. I didn't want to deal with Aimee today. I had too much to do. I dropped the heavy canvas bag full of hooks on the booth's wooden floor. It landed with a thud and a series of clanks. Aaron had installed a peg board on one wall. The hooks would fit into the holes and display Aunt Grace's collars, harnesses, leashes, training bags, and bandanas, and Maeve's dog cookie bags.

"I need to go back to the car to get the tables." Maybe Aimee would be gone by the time I got back. "Can you and Bubbles stay right here so I don't have to worry about you?"

She nodded. "I'll start with the hooks."

I'd probably have to rearrange them later, but it would keep her busy. "Go ahead."

Focusing on carrying two folding tables back to the booth and juggling a broom, I didn't notice Aimee standing by my door until it was too late to ignore her.

She reached out and took the broom from me.

I wrestled the tables past her and into the booth, then snatched the broom from her. "What are you doing here?"

Neve lined up hooks carefully with the holes in the pegboard. Bubbles had moved to Aimee's side and licked at her hand.

Aimee rested a shoulder casually against the door jamb, petting Bubbles. "I'll be around a lot, so get used to it. Lara asked me to run her booth this year, and I was checking out how much space we had. Plus, Oliver wanted me to take measurements for the vineyard's booth."

I leaned the tables against the wall and they landed with a hard slam that made Bubbles jump, but Aimee didn't even flinch, just tilted her head and raised her eyebrows as if unimpressed.

"Sorry, girl," I told Bubbles and scratched her behind the ears.

Aimee couldn't afford a donation to the dog shelter but she could afford to decorate the vineyard's booth. It seemed par for the course. She'd had her priorities wrong back in high school and hadn't changed.

She chewed at her upper lip, fingers digging deep into Bubbles' hair. "Is this the center's booth?"

"The dog shelter's. We need to find new homes for at least a dozen dogs. Or else ..." I shrugged as if no big deal but it was the biggest deal for me. Every dog I couldn't save was a personal failure. "If they don't make enough money to see them through the winter, then the shelter will have to close permanently."

"I've made a poster for Phoebe, and I'm going to help her take better photos of the dogs looking for homes." She looked so smug at her tiny effort that I wanted to slug her. "She said you planned on writing a story for each."

I had to admit, though, that good photos would help the dogs. I had a board on which I planned to place the photos and stories to attract attention. I'd also made some Adopted stickers to place over each adopted dog's photo. That would, hopefully, bring some FOMO. "Since when are you handy with a camera?"

"Since it was my minor."

"Okay, well, I'll let you get back to it." I nodded toward the pegboard. "I need to get everything set and get back to the center."

"Lark ..." Aimee inhaled and pinched her lips flat, hands balling at her sides. "I am truly sorry—"

"Let's not start with that again."

"I'm really trying—"

"There's nothing you could do to—"

Aimee growled. "You're so stubborn! So unreasonable. You never used to be such a b—"

"Watch it." I placed my hands over Neve's ears. "Vulnerable child here."

"You started it." Her jaw worked and the sheen of tears filled her eyes. At her side, Bubbles whined.

"No, *you* started it."

Aimee let out a bitter laugh. "Fine, you know what. You win. You get to keep your anger and resentment and hold it against me for the rest of my life. I can move on. I can make different choices." She lifted a hand, as if trying to breach a void, then thinking better of it, dropped it. "But you, you're stuck in the past."

She stalked away, and Bubbles started to follow her, but I called my dog back. Halfway to her booth, one ankle rolled and Aimee stumbled. She caught herself and, for a moment, just stood there, shoulders hunched, before straightening and continuing as if nothing had happened.

The crisp autumn air did nothing to cool the heat burning my cheeks. Pulse ticking at my throat, I swiped a stray strand of hair behind my ear. With a determined pivot, I turned back to the pegboard, hooking hook after hook into the holes like a crazed machine.

At my side, Neve continued to carefully place her hooks, her focus determined. "Why is the lady so sad?"

I swallowed hard, thinking back to the complete shattering

of my heart all those years ago. *Because she wants me to forgive her for something unforgiveable.*

Across the way, Aimee had stopped to talk with an older woman pulling a cart of homemade candles. The woman touched Aimee's arm and said something. Aimee laughed, her face softening in a way I remembered from our childhood.

She was moving on. She was going to make a life here.

Without me.

And I was ... still stuck.

Neve tugged on my sleeve. "You're sad, too."

"I am. She used to be my best friend."

Neve nodded in a way that spoke of wisdom. "When my best friend Riley moved, I was really sad. At first, she wrote me emails every day. But then, she stopped, and I hated her. Grandma said that holding a grudge was like drinking poison and expecting the other person to get sick."

"Your grandma is a smart lady." I glanced at Aimee's booth, expecting her to still be there, but she was gone—leaving an odd emptiness.

I inhaled the tears threatening to spill. Neve was right. My anger and resentment came from deep hurt. But by keeping them alive and simmering, I was only hurting myself.

That didn't mean I knew how to stop.

14

———

On Friday, after the influx of daycare dogs, Phoebe breezed into the Canine Center, the door swinging shut behind her with a *clunk*. The air carried the scent of dog toes, kibble and the sweetness of today's peanut butter treats. Dogs barked happily in the background, their feet thumping on the floor as they played with Rae, whose laughter rang out like a handful of small bells.

Phoebe dropped her cavernous bag onto the counter and plucked out a thick file. "I don't have much time, but I wanted to drop these off."

The file hit the counter with a dull thud. Curious, I flipped it open, fingers brushing over the glossy photo. That first image stopped me cold. A black Lab—no, a *perfect* portrait of a black Lab—stared back at me, eyes soulful, expression filled with something so raw and real that my breath caught. So different from the prison mugshot Phoebe had taken of him last week. "Wow!"

"Yeah, that's what I said." Phoebe clucked her tongue. "Your friend Aimee—"

"She's not my friend." The words came out too fast, but I didn't take them back.

Phoebe raised a brow, but continued, "—took these yesterday. She spent all day with the dogs, taking her time. I don't know how she did it, but she captured each dog's personality." Phoebe let out a rocky laugh, shaking her head. "Makes me want to adopt a dog."

That was saying something. Given that, like me, Phoebe already fostered too many dogs. We both knew wanting and should were two different things.

She tapped an impatient hand against the counter. "We need to get those auction baskets together. Tonight? My place?"

I dragged my gaze away from the photo of the black Lab, willing my brain to switch gears. "Depends on if my nighttime helper shows up. If not, we could do it here."

Phoebe gave one sharp nod. "Sounds like a plan."

At the sound of the door slamming, I turned my attention back to the file, flipping through the images. Phoebe was right. These shots were excellent. Some had dreamy, blurred backgrounds, making the dogs look as if they belonged in a magazine spread. Some captured dogs mid-motion, ears flapping, tongues lolling with joy. Every single photo was taken at dog height, not from above, meaning Aimee had to get down on the ground in her fancy clothes just to get the right shot.

My jaw tightened. How could someone who could betray her best friend take such insightful photos? How could someone so untrustworthy see the heart of these dogs so clearly?

I snapped the file shut harder than necessary. Aimee didn't matter. Only the dogs.

"Oh my god! Those eyes!"

I startled, hand flying to my chest. Rae stood behind me, grinning. "Sorry, thought you heard me." She nodded toward the folder. "Those pictures are awesome."

"They are."

She hooked a thumb over her shoulder. "I'm taking the dogs out for their potty breaks. Keep an ear out?"

I nodded, still feeling the lingering effects of the photos. They *would* help. That was what mattered. I needed to find time to go to the shelter and sit with each dog to get their stories, and make sure those images worked as hard as possible to get them adopted.

I stuffed the file in my bag and sighed. My body ached for rest, but that wouldn't come any time soon.

"Rae?"

"Yeah?" came her answer from somewhere in the back.

"I have to leave for a bit."

"Okay. But I have to go by three. I have a class at four."

"I'll be back."

That left me about four hours to figure out how to build dog suites, get the supplies, and squeeze in a training session with Max and Caleb.

The thought exhausted me.

But it also exhilarated me.

CALEB MET us at the lumber yard where he practiced having Max heel on a loose leash amid the distraction of forklifts, carts and people, while I tried to figure out what I needed to build the dog suites.

As I stared at a whole rack of screws and nails, Caleb reached out and stroked the skin between my eyes, making me jerk back from his touch. The warmth of his fingers lingered, unexpected and grounding, and I stupidly wished he'd do it again.

"What's making you frown so?" As he studied me, his own brow furrowed.

I sidestepped, pretending to have an eager interest in a package of screws. "I'm not a carpenter and I need to build six dog suites at the new space. I want them to be portable so I can use them in whatever permanent spot I find."

"That's smart."

Part of me warmed at the compliment, a silly flicker of pleasure I quickly doused with a no-big-deal shrug. "I've already asked Aaron for too many favors. I have to figure out how to do this myself." I waved some papers. "I found these plans online, but some of these supplies, I have no idea what they look like. And the wood ..." I whistled. "Way more expensive than I imagined."

"Let me see." Caleb snatched the papers from my hand and studied the plans. Max sat by Caleb's feet, looking up at him with adoration, the kind I told myself I didn't envy.

"You need something temporary, right?" Caleb took my pen.

"Something transferable would be better."

He looked up from the papers and deep into my eyes, making heat flood my insides like a sauna. "But what you need right now is something to separate the dogs while you look for new space."

I nodded. "They deserve a cozy, safe space to sleep, especially if they're missing their owners."

"We can build them from old pallets." Caleb sketched alterations to the plan while Max batted a paw at his leg for attention. "That would cost you nothing for the wood."

I opened my mouth, but he stopped me with hand. "I know where to find some for free."

"My favorite price."

"All you'd need is to get are wood screws, and then some stain or paint—I can get you rejects from the store at low cost—and some hinges and latches for the doors." He smiled, the first genuine smile I'd seen since he'd come to the center. "I'll even give you the friends-and-family discount."

"Really?" That sounded too good to be true.

He narrowed his gaze as if searching for something in his memory. "I might still have some old rubber mats you could use to cushion the floor."

I stuffed my hands in my jeans pockets, torn. The idea was good, incredible actually, and yet my *Yes* and *Thank you* stuck in my throat. As if sensing my hesitation, Max bopped my leg with his nose. I reached down to pet him, grateful for the distraction.

Max gave a soft whine. *"Good guy."*

He is.

"I'm offering to help you, Lark." He folded the plans and stuffed them in his jacket pocket. Max gave a woof, and Caleb unconsciously reached down to pet his head.

I frowned at him again. "Why?"

"You're helping me." He reached out and smoothed the ridges of my frown once more. I wanted to lean into his touch, but stayed still, heart knocking against my ribs.

"Selfishly." I jerked my chin in Max's direction, breaking our connection. "Because Max desperately needs a permanent home. Or he could end up ..." I put a hand over my mouth and whispered, "... *euthanized.*"

"You never mentioned that."

"I want you to want Max. He's been through a lot. He deserves someone who wants him for him, not as an obligation." I crouched down and petted Max, who licked my hand. "And you're too stubborn to see you two belong together."

"I—" Caleb started, then stopped. His face shuttered, and just like that, the warmth between us disappeared like fog in morning sun.

"What?" I pressed. If I could understand why he was so against taking care of Max, I could allay his fears.

He hesitated, something wavered in his eyes—something raw and primal. For a second, it seemed as if he might tell me.

Instead, he handed me Max's leash. "No matter what. I'll still help you."

The thought that he might reject Max after the connection they'd built hurt. And yet, the thought of working with him to build the dog suites was much too pleasant.

Caleb turned away, and Max let out a pleading whine. "*My guy.*"

I stared at Caleb's retreating back, a thousand questions clogging my throat. *Look back!*

And then, as he reached the door, he did.

He lingered, one hand braced against the door frame, his shoulders rising. A muscle ticked in his jaw.

"I'll see you tomorrow after work," he finally said, voice like rusted steel.

I sucked in a breath, confused as to whether he'd made a promise or if he'd offered a warning.

Then he was gone, and Max and I were left standing there. What had just happened?

15

W hile I was checking out daycare dogs, the center's phone rang. "Stoneley Canine Center. How can I help you?"

"I'm looking for Lark Eamon," came a voice that sounded young, like a teenager's.

My fingers tensed on the receiver. "You've found her."

"This is Sabrina Sands from the *Tri-Town Tribune*, and we'd like to run an article about the Adopt-a-Thon next weekend."

"That would be terrific." I exhaled, relaxing my shoulders. I stepped aside so Bo could finish checking out the dogs. "We can use all the publicity we can get. So many dogs need good homes."

"I wanted to take a different angle."

On their own, the words weren't alarming, but something about her tone, the eagerness of it, sent a shiver of unease through me.

"Oh?" I kept my voice neutral.

"Show how you're the best person to place these dogs because of your ability to talk to them."

The hum of the front desk computer, the pad of dog paws

against the linoleum, the barks of joy, all got sharper, louder, making my mind buzz. This gift, this curse, was going to ruin me again. *Stay calm. Stay in control.*

I let out a rough laugh. "If I could actually talk to dogs, I'd be making a fortune on TV instead of running a dog center in the middle of nowhere New Hampshire."

"Oh, I don't know." Sabrina's voice carried a teasing lilt, but I didn't trust it. "A fortune's nice. But I hear your style's more into saving dogs."

I kept my voice steady, but my pulse galloped like a chased dog. "Well, one needs money to save dogs ..."

I let the silence deepen, hoping she'd get the hint and change the subject.

"I have it from a reliable source that you can hear dogs' thoughts."

My whole body turned to ice. Who? The question raced through my mind, chased by even worse ones. How long before the rumor spread through town once more? Would I lose my customers? My business? "What source would that be?"

"Confidential source."

Had Aimee betrayed me again? "For an interview about shelter dogs?"

A sharp bark interrupted our conversation. Diesel, a yellow Lab, pounced on me, front paws landing on my chest, pushing me back a step before I caught myself. *"Lark! Lark! Wanna cookie!"*

I reached into the treat jar, gave him a cookie and shooed him back to his owner.

"What was that?" Sabrina's tone sharpened as if she'd landed a fish on her hook.

"What was what?"

"That noise. It sounded like a dog talking to you."

There was no way she could have heard Diesel, so I forced lightness into my voice. "Ha-ha, that's just Diesel. He barks for a cookie before he goes home. He did it once, so now it's tradition."

She didn't say anything, but I could almost hear her mental gears turning. "Huh."

One syllable stretched tight with doubt.

I pressed on, voice breezy. "I hate to disappoint you, but I just read dogs' body language well. Always have."

A longer pause. A rustle as if she were jotting something down.

She's not going to let this go.

Behind me, owners greeted their dogs, tails thumped against the desk, and Bo answered questions about the dogs' days. But all I could hear was the throb of my own pulse.

Sabrina sighed. "Oh. Well, that's disappointing."

Relief softened the tension in my chest.

Then she added, "Guess there's no real story there."

And just like that, mid-exhale, the relief evaporated.

If she didn't write the article, the shelter would lose a good shot at much-needed publicity.

I scrambled. "Wait—so you're not going to write about the Adopt-a-Thon?" She *had* to understand just how dire the situation was. "The shelter really needs the coverage. If we don't adopt out at least twelve dogs, some of the older or infirm dogs will be put down."

"Put down?" She gulped.

I kept going, willing her to help the dogs. "And if the auction doesn't make enough money to cover feed, vet bills and heat for the winter, the shelter will have to shut down. Permanently." I softened my tone. "That's the real story, Sabrina. Not me. The dogs."

A pause. "Oh—"

I pounced on her hesitation. "Here's Phoebe Flowers' number." I rattled off her cell phone. "She runs the Tri-Town

Dog Shelter in Stoneley. She'll have all the information you need to write a fantastic article."

"Um, okay …" The clicking of a pen on and off came through the line. "Are you sure you can't talk to dogs?"

Careful. Don't give her even a hint. I let out an easy chuckle. "I can talk to them, but they don't talk back."

"Okay, well, thanks." Her voice held enough disappointment to overflow a bucket.

I set the phone down and let out a slow breath. Had I dodged a bullet? But if Sabrina wanted her story, she could keep digging.

Bo shot me a curious glance from the front desk. "Everything okay?"

I nodded. Too quickly. Too automatically.

As my mind sorted through the possibilities, my cell phone vibrated in my pocket. I swallowed hard. The reporter wouldn't call back this soon, would she? She couldn't. She didn't have my personal number.

The phone vibrated again as if it were a rattler about to strike.

I hesitated and pulled it out of my pocket.

Unknown number. Possible spam, my phone warned.

I put the phone away. I'd had enough surprises today.

Should I have said yes to the interview, then skirted around the dog-talk questions, focusing her back on the dogs?

I'd let my fear of being called crazy, of being ridiculed and ostracized all over again get in the way of the dogs' welfare. That wasn't like me. Because Sabrina got one thing right: to me, the dogs were more important than money.

I had to fix this. Somehow.

I had to make sure the dogs got their article.

~

LATER THAT EVENING, surrounded by baskets, a rainbow of paper shreds and bows, clear cellophane wrappers, and what looked like a ton of basket stuffers for the auction, Phoebe and I sat on the floor of the reception area at the Canine Center. The air smelled of coffee from Phoebe's giant travel mug, cinnamon and ginger from the cookies Mom had dropped off earlier—leftovers from her book club meeting—and the ever-present scent of dog.

Outside, the wind rattled the Welcome sign against the door, and cold seeped beneath the tattered weatherstripping. The kind of cold that made everything feel lonelier when you were by yourself. Having Phoebe here was nice.

Phoebe, with her usual over-caffeinated energy, arranged and rearranged the contents of her breakfast-themed basket. "So, what's the beef between you and Aimee?"

My hands stilled for a moment before fluffing the green paper shreds in my basket, careful not to look up. "No beef. Just a friendship that ran its course. Forks in the road and all that."

"Uh-huh." Phoebe finished stuffing her basket with jams, jellies and scone mixes and reached for a large cellophane bag. "She had nothing but nice things to say about you."

A short laugh slipped out before I could stop it. "So, there you go. You know that's not true."

She tilted her head, watching me as if I were a puzzle she was trying to solve. "Why do you do that?"

"Do what?"

"Put yourself down all the time."

I smoothed the cellophane over my basket, pretending to focus on getting the folds just right. "Old habit, I guess."

But that wasn't the whole truth. Reality was much messier. When you heard enough versions of why you weren't good enough, they started to feel like fact.

Phoebe blew a raspberry. "Well, stop it. It's not becoming."

I snorted. "That's the nicest way anyone's ever told me to shut up."

She grinned, grabbing a spool of orange ribbon. "I didn't think you liked me."

That threw me. "What? What makes you think that?"

"You're always so short with me."

My fingers fumbled the bow I was trying to tie. "I thought that was you."

She huffed a laugh. "Yeah, my husband keeps telling me I have a 'tone' that puts people off. In my previous life, I was a manager, supervising a group of men who resented a female boss." She shook her head. "I guess I have an old habit, too."

She put the breakfast basket on the table and reached for an empty wicker basket. "I wouldn't have asked you to help with something as important as the Adopt-a-Thon unless I liked you and trusted you."

I blinked, thrown again. She liked me?

Could I trust that? Could I trust anyone?

"Thank you," I said, the words coming out like caution lights. "That means a lot to me."

Phoebe shifted her attention to the pile of donations, choosing a self-care theme for her next basket. "It's tough making new friends as an adult. I've met a lot of people since Nick and I moved here five years ago, but because I spend so much time at the shelter ..." She lifted a shoulder and let it drop. "I haven't really made any friends."

"Same here." The words slipped out before I'd quite decided if I wanted to say them. I hesitated, feeling the weight of loneliness pressing against my chest. "I mostly say hi and bye to people, so not much chance to form friendships."

I didn't add the rest—that trust felt like a risk I wasn't sure I could take. I'd already been burned once. I didn't want to feel that kind of hurt again.

Phoebe frowned. "But you've lived here for all of your life. Surely you have friends."

The sad truth was that I didn't. "A lot of people moved away. Differing interests took us down separate paths."

Phoebe let out a breath, arranging soaps and lotions into her basket as if they were dominoes that would topple if she let one drop. "I thought it was just me." She glanced up, a small, hopeful smile forming. "This is nice, though, right?"

I opened my mouth to answer, but before I could get there, a rustling came from the hallway to the overnight suites. Sadie, my pit bull mix foster, peeked around the corner. I'd been working with her for months. Phoebe had rescued her from a bad situation, but she still wasn't comfortable around people.

"Hey, pretty girl." I reached in my pocket for a treat. She inched forward, ears perked, tail giving a tentative wag. "Come say hello to Phoebe."

Phoebe smiled like a proud parent. "She's getting braver."

"She is." Head low, Sadie took another slow step toward us, then stopped, staring at us as if Phoebe was a predator and she was prey. I tossed a few treats her way and she laid down, crunching each while staying vigilant.

I could hear her fear buzzing in her mind. After all the time I'd spent with her, she still wondered if she was safe here.

I understood how she felt.

Phoebe sighed and stretched out her short legs, one hiking boot hit a spool of ribbon and sent it rolling. Sadie scrabbled up and retreated. "Sadie, sorry, I didn't mean to scare you." Phoebe said. "Come back."

"She will. She's a treat mooch."

Phoebe rolled her shoulders. "We should do this more often."

"Running an Adopt-a-Thon more than once a year?" I teased, needing to lighten the moment.

She smirked. "Doing something fun together." Her voice

hitched as if the words were prickly. "I've been thinking of doing one of those paint-and-sip workshops at the collaborative in Brighton. Any interest?"

I hesitated. Was this one of those polite invites people didn't actually expect you to accept?

Catching my hesitation, Phoebe waved a hand. "No pressure. I just thought it might be fun."

It would be fun. And maybe that's what scared me. "I saw they had a workshop to make a hummingbird feeder from wine bottles."

Her smile returned, reaching all the way to her eyes. "Practical and pretty. The best of both worlds."

"Well, I'm not exactly the best at artsy stuff, but I wouldn't mind trying."

"It's a date then."

For a second, neither of us said anything. Then Phoebe reached toward the unspooled purple ribbon and handed it to me. "Goes with all those purple dog things in your basket."

A small gesture that, for some reason, caught me off guard.

A warmth settled in my chest. It felt good to have someone want to spend time with me. Sadie reappeared, army-crawling a bit closer, nose stretching out toward the treats in my pocket.

Maybe friendship was like that, one tiny army-crawl forward at a time.

I offered Sadie a treat just out of reach. She crawled closer, and I rewarded her. "Did Sabrina Sands from the *Tri-Town Tribune* ever call you?"

"Was she supposed to?"

"She wanted to write an article about the Adopt-a-Thon, and I told her you were the best person to ask because you had all the information."

Phoebe let out a long breath. "We could definitely use the publicity. I'll reach out to her."

She got up and stretched her arms over her head. "I need a break. Want anything?"

I glanced at the mess of donations still waiting for baskets. At this rate, we'd be here all night. "I should keep going."

She disappeared into the office behind the reception desk. A few minutes later, she returned with two mugs, setting one down next to me before sinking back onto the floor. "Thought you could use a pick-me-up."

I blinked, glancing at my favorite dog paw mug. Steam curled from the surface, carrying the scent of peppermint.

"Thanks." I wrapped my fingers around the warmth.

Maybe, just maybe, I could let myself believe in friendship again.

16

After a mad day of ping-ponging between taking care of dogs and checking items off my Adopt-a-Thon list, I was ready for some food and an early night. But I'd told Caleb I'd meet him at the Country Store for the building supplies he'd gathered for me, and I was running late.

Max rode in the back, tail beating a tattoo against the vinyl of the seat. *"Where we goin'? What're we doin'? My guy?"*

"We're meeting him at the store, then going to the new space to build some dog suites."

"Bacon?"

"Not today, Max."

"Wrrr," he grumbled.

I parked in the alleyway between stores. When Max saw Caleb, he happy-barked.

"You'll want to tone that down. Caleb doesn't like loud noises."

"Noises? What noises?"

"Barking."

"Oh." Max switched to small yips instead.

Caleb pulled open the tailgate to my old station wagon and loaded the back with paint cans, brushes, rubber mats, and hardware. By the time I reached the tailgate, he'd already stowed everything away. Before I could say anything, he slammed the tailgate down, biceps flexing. *Nice*, I thought, then shook the thought away. *Not appropriate, Lark.*

Our gazes met and something flared in his eyes. "I'll meet you there."

"I wish you'd let me give you a ride," I shouted to his back. "I don't like you riding out there in the dark."

He glanced at me over his shoulder, mouth quirking into a teasing grin. "Worried about me?"

"As a matter of fact ..."

His face sobered. "Don't. I'll be fine."

As if to prove his point, he mounted his bike and disappeared down the road in a blur of silver reflective material, spinning lights on the spokes of his wheels, and the bob of his bike light illuminating the way.

My hands gripped the steering wheel more tightly than necessary. Why was he so stubborn?

"What am I going to do about this car phobia?" How could he take care of Max if he refused to drive or even ride in a car? How would he get Max to the vet? Or to any of the functions where Max could help him?

Max licked my ear—as if a good lick was the answer to everything. I laughed, imagining Caleb's reaction to me licking his cheek. Heat crept up my neck at the thought of being so close, of smelling his soap and cedar scent ... of leaning into him. "Yeah, that wouldn't go over well."

At the old daycare, to keep my mind from going to places I didn't want it to, I forced myself to focus on unloading the supplies. Max stood guard on the concrete pad, staring at the road for Caleb's arrival. Someone had already delivered a stack of wooden pallets, a saw and table and a set of plastic sawhorses and left them in the reception area, creating a maze to get to the hallway.

Once done piling supplies into the kennel room, I studied Caleb's revised plans for the suite. Max's happy barks filled the night. He trotted in behind Caleb. *"He's here. He's here."*

Caleb dropped his backpack on the reception desk, took off his jacket, then picked up the suite plan, and leaned against the counter. His T-shirt, damp with sweat, clung to his pecs. I had to look away.

Caleb pushed off the counter. "Let's go look at the space."

In the room, he made a full turn, then took out a measuring tape from his pocket. "How many suites do you want?"

"Want and will settle for are two different things." My gaze swept the room. "I think we can comfortably fit six in here."

The measuring tape retreated back in its casing with a *click-clack* noise. "Yeah, that's about the max."

"I don't want the suites to feel confining, but more like their own private Eden."

He chuckled and the sound warmed my chest. "You're not asking much from wood and screws."

I pointed at all the supplies I'd piled in the middle of the room. "You're forgetting paint, rubber mats and, eventually, comfy beds."

He gave me a strange look that had me finding reasons to look anywhere but at him. "You always did care about making dogs feel at home."

Throat burning from his quiet words of praise, I shrugged a shoulder. "So where do we start?"

"Know how to use a circular saw?"

"Not even a little bit."

"Okay, you measure ..." He scribbled down measurements. "I'll cut."

"Measure twice, cut once."

He gave me a thumb's up, fingers flexing around the measuring tape as if grounding himself. Back at the reception area, he rifled through the stack of pallets, picking out the nicest ones. "We'll use those for the walls that face the room." He gave me a wry smile. "I know how you like things to look pretty."

I stuck my tongue out at him. I did like for things to look nice. "Nothing wrong with liking a bit of color and fun."

"Nothing wrong, at all." He handed me the tape measure, his fingers warm against mine, stirring up heat low in my belly.

You're reading things that aren't there, Lark.

Caleb started another pile. Max sniffed at the wood as if it contained urgent messages he had to decipher. "We'll use these for the frames."

Caleb pulled nails from the pallet stringers, then straightened back up. "Okay, start measuring for the bases. I'll get the saw set up."

We worked in companionable silence, to the symphony of whining saws and the grinding of drills, measuring and cutting. Soon the air filled with the scent of sawdust and sweat. Max dogged Caleb, determined to stick by his guy, and Caleb played keep away to shield Max from harm. My throat worked. They were bonding and didn't even realize it. Soon, I thought, soon Caleb will want Max with him every day.

Eventually, Max got bored of getting sawdust all over him. He found a corner with a painting tarp, sneezed, and made himself a nest.

Caleb showed me how to use a drill to pre-drill holes to make a simple frame. He screwed in a center support and angle clamps to keep everything square. His nearness made it difficult to concentrate on his instruction. I never realized how much I liked the scent of cedar.

Together, we moved the frame to the kennel room, Max insisting on getting in the way.

While Caleb worked on the other five frames, I rough cleaned the wall wood with a sander. Before long, the walls came up. Caleb constantly checked they were square in all directions. He marked out a door opening for the front.

"Let's take a break."

I should have thought of bringing something to feed him. He'd worked so hard that a sheen of sweat had formed on his forehead. All I had to offer him was the water and granola bars I kept in the car in case of emergency. They were probably stale; I couldn't remember when I'd put them in the emergency kit.

I took the broom leaning against the wall and swept sawdust into a dustpan. "Let me take you out to dinner."

"We're almost done." He nodded toward the reception area. "Mom packed me a snack. And if I know Mom, she probably put enough food in there for half the village."

Mrs. Singer did like to feed people. Caleb had often arrived at our house for play dates, arms laden with baked goods.

We sat on the floor, cross-legged. Max stretched out across Caleb's lap. As soon as Max pressed against Caleb's thighs, Caleb's whole body sighed into relaxation, making me smile.

The roast beef sandwiches with their sharp bite of horseradish sauce, tomatoes and lettuce hit the spot. I moaned. He stared at me.

"What?" I swiped a hand across my cheeks. "Do I have something on my face?"

He chuckled, his gaze lingering on my lips a beat too long. "I'm just enjoying you enjoying that sandwich."

Heat invaded my cheeks. "I guess I was hungrier than I thought. Next time, dinner's on me."

"Next time," he said, voice rich and deep, like the whiskey

Dad liked to drink on dark winter nights. It felt like a promise —and a question.

Chewing slowly on his sandwich, he stroked Max's back, and Max puddled on his lap, sighing in his sleep. I wanted to ask what had happened in Seattle, but didn't dare break the companionable mood between us.

Instead, I tried to creak open the door to his fortress. "What did you do in Seattle?"

He scoffed. "You mean, the Brighton rumor mill didn't keep you informed?"

"I quit listening a long time ago."

He glanced at me, something unreadable flashing across his face before he looked out the window as if he could see all the way to Seattle. "I worked for a company that made innovative medical devices."

"Did you like it?"

"Most of the time." He crooked a shoulder. Max cracked an eye open, then closed it again. "The technology their engineers created is saving a lot of lives."

"But ..."

He took a bite of sandwich and chewed methodically. Buying himself time? "Something was missing."

"And you're finding it here?" I couldn't help the wistful note, a note I wished I could take back when his gaze locked with mine. Staring right into me as if he could see past all the layers I'd built over the years. Then something else ... loneliness? Whatever it was pulled strings of yearning on my heart.

"I—" He squeezed the nape of his neck with a hand. "I'm trying."

"You hadn't planned on coming back."

"Dad needed me. And the timing worked out." The shutters falling over his eyes told me not to push.

I studied my sandwich, examining the layers like a geologist. I hadn't felt this kind of longing in ages. And I had no idea what to do with it. I certainly couldn't trust it. And Caleb couldn't trust me. I'd lied to him about hearing the dogs. As I learned the hard way, a relationship without trust couldn't survive.

A part of me had gone cold after Aimee's betrayal. I'd never expected to care for anyone again. Not this way. And this unexpected thawing stung, leaving me raw and exposed.

"What about you?" He reached for one of the water bottles on the floor between us. "You never left."

"I couldn't." Appetite gone, I wrapped what was left of the sandwich, then wished I hadn't because now I didn't know what to do with my hands. "Not after Liam left the way he did, not staying in touch with Mom. Every day he doesn't answer a text or send an email breaks her heart all over again." I sent him a pleading look, hoping for what, I wasn't sure—understanding? Reassurance? An offer I shouldn't ask for? "Maybe he'd listen to you."

"I'll try." He leaned forward and tucked a stray strand of hair behind my ear. His fingers lingered on the pulse at my throat, making it jump like a trapped bird.

I cleared my throat. "What's left?"

He let his hand fall away, a slow, reluctant move. "We'll attach three of the suites together and anchor them to one wall and do the same on the other side of the room."

Stretching his arms up, he yawned, revealing inches of taut stomach. I curled my fingers, fighting the impulse to reach out and touch him. "Then we'll call it a night. After that, all that's left will be the finishing touches. Painting and sealing."

His gaze traveled down the hall. "I was thinking I might have something at the store that we can use for a door so that the dogs can see out and not feel caged but still stay contained."

"That would be great."

As we worked, the mood between us sparked like the air before a storm. Every accidental touch a flash of lightning.

Every inadvertent contact a rumble of thunder. Outside, the clouds thickened against the night sky and the air turned thick with the scent of rain.

By the time we were done, real rain had arrived, belting against the roof in heavy sheets, turning the driveway into a shimmering river.

"Please, Caleb, let me drive you home. This weather isn't safe."

He rubbed a hand over his jaw. "It's all good."

"You'll get hypothermia."

He pulled on his reflective jacket. "I don't need you to worry about me."

"Too late."

His gaze met mine. Then he exhaled and turned away, hiking his backpack over his shoulders.

Why did he have to be so difficult?

"Fine." I shoved my arms into my coat. Max twirling around both our feet, getting in the way. "Then I'm going to follow you until I know you got home safe."

He pulled on his gloves and helmet and rolled his eyes but didn't argue.

True to my word, I followed him all the way to his tiny house. Once there, I rolled down the window. "Want Max to spend the night?"

"*Yes! Yes!*" Max barked, tail circling like a whirligig.

Caleb hesitated. Long enough for my heart to catch. Then, without a word, he lifted a hand in farewell and disappeared inside. The click of the lock echoed in the rain.

I'd pushed him too hard.

Rain lashed against my windshield, streaking the glass, blurring the glow of his porch light until the next swipe of the wipers.

I should drive away, let it go.

Instead, I lingered a moment longer, waiting for a sign that he might change his mind.

But the curtain never twitched. And the door never opened. My phone never rang.

"*Why?*" Max whined. "*Why?*"

"I don't know, Max."

With a sigh, I put the car in gear. We couldn't do this push-and-pull for Max much longer.

The Adopt-a-Thon was less than a week away.

17

———

I leaned against the brick side of the Country Store next to Caleb's bicycle, hoping to intercept him on his way home. Max sat patiently at my feet, staring at the door as if he could make it open faster.

Max's tail sweeping the pavement announced Caleb's arrival.

He opened the door and blinked. "What are you doing here?"

I waggled my eyebrows. "Kidnapping you."

He glanced down at Max and said, "Is this legal?"

"*Yes!*" Max barked and wagged his tail so hard, his whole rear end moved.

"I'm taking you to dinner for all the work you've done on the sleep suites at the new center."

A smile twitched at the corner of his mouth. "Boxed mac 'n cheese?"

I laughed. "Better. Bob's House. They have the best burgers in town."

He took in a long breath and, for a second, I thought he'd refuse. "How can I say no to the best burger in town?"

Relief settled in my chest. I'd planned a simple training session, just me and Caleb and Max. No surprises. And on Sunday, the place should be relatively empty.

We headed down the sidewalk to the brewpub, our feet ringing in time against the concrete.

"Are dogs allowed inside?" Caleb asked, hands in his jacket pockets, where I suspected he held them in tight fists.

"Kenny has two rescues that are official mascots for the place, and customers can let their dogs in the designated play area while their owners eat." I patted the side of my bag where I'd stowed a training vest. "But Max, as a service-dog-in-training, will get to sit under the table."

Caleb's jaw worked. "Should've known you were bamboozling me."

"Bamboozling? That's an odd word."

"For an odd girl."

For some reason, coming from Caleb, the word odd sounded like a compliment. "Yep, that's me, odd."

"I meant it in a nice way."

"How is *odd* nice in any way?"

He lifted a shoulder, let if fall. "It's different and different ... warrants attention."

"Good attention?"

"Definitely."

I pushed open the heavy door of the brewpub, Max trotting obediently at my side. The place buzzed with Friday-night energy—even though it was only Sunday—laughter, clinking glasses, and the rich scent of sizzling burgers filled the air. The warmth inside contrasted sharply with the crisp night air we'd just left, making my skin prickle.

"Sorry, I didn't expect this many people." I scoured the room for an empty table and found none. "Probably because of the Pumpkin Festival. Or leaf peeping. We can go elsewhere, if you want."

He squared his shoulders. "This is fine."

A familiar voice sliced through the hum of conversation, sending an uneasy ripple down my spice.

"Lark!"

I groaned. Aimee.

My grip tightened on Max's leash. Aimee sat at a corner table, arm's length away. How had I not seen her? I recognized the man next to her from the wedding photo on her desk. He was even more handsome in real life, his face open, his eyes kind. He wore an easy glow of joy just under his skin, as if he was simply ... good.

Aimee's eyes held a hopeful expression that made me want to turn around and leave. Fast. The air between us thickened with unsaid words and lingering wounds.

"Looks like there's not a free table in sight." Oliver's tone was light, oblivious to the storm between Aimee and me. He grinned at Caleb. "Why don't you join us?"

My mouth opened, a refusal forming, but Caleb beat me. "Thanks. That'd be great."

Aimee nudged out the empty chair beside her, but I slid into the one next to Caleb instead. I had Max lie down at my feet. The cold wood of the chair, rigid beneath me, stiffened my spine. My muscles tensed even as I willed myself to put on a smile. "It's nice to finally meet you, Oliver."

I introduced Caleb and Max. "He's in training right now."

"Is that why he's under the table?" Aimee asked.

I nodded. "Service dogs stay under the table, so service staff and other customers won't trip over them. Keeps everyone safe."

"You always did care about making a difference." Aimee twisted a napkin on her lap as if she too wasn't sure how to deal with the barricade of tension between us.

"I still do." I turned my smile onto Oliver. "That's why I asked about a donation to the shelter's fundraiser."

Oliver nodded in a way that said he cared. "The fundraiser sounds like a huge deal. Aimee's told me how much work you've put into it. I really wish we could've made a bigger contribution. But with all the renovations ..."

I asked Oliver about how the upgrades to the vineyard were coming along. My smile was too wide, and I was trying too hard to pretend a wall didn't exist between me and Aimee.

We ordered. Oliver regaled us with his renovation adventures. I could see how Aimee had fallen for him. That kindness and openness were genuine. As was his charm. Aimee laughed at something her husband said, the sound familiar and light— the echo of something lost. For the briefest moment, the warmth of the past threatened to thaw the ice in my chest.

"You wouldn't believe what I found in the barn," Oliver said, as our food arrived. "I was going through an old desk tucked in the attic and found a locked drawer. I jiggled the lock. And there it was. A brass urn labeled 'Mr. Radcliffe.' I opened it and found ashes, and I thought, oh my God, someone forgot their ancestor. I called the previous owners and they had no idea who that was. So I did more digging." His laughter was round and rolling and infectious. "You'll never guess."

"Well," I said, picking up a French fry. "Don't keep us in suspense. Who?"

"A horse."

"A horse?" I said.

Oliver shook his head as if he still didn't believe the answer. "Apparently, the owner before the Thornes kept horses in the barn, and Mr. Radcliffe was his favorite one. He wanted the horse's ashes buried with him when he died but no one could find the urn."

"So what did you do?" Caleb looked at his burger as if it were an alien creature before taking a bite.

"Found out where he was buried and asked the cemetery

caretaker if he could bury the urn with Mr. Radcliffe's ashes with Mr. Moody as per his wishes."

Aimee reached for Oliver's hand and beamed at him, glowing with love. He gave her the same look back. A nip of envy pinched at me. "He reunited two lost souls."

Beside me, Caleb shifted his beer from one hand to the other. The press of bodies, the clatter of silverware, the bursts of raucous laughter were closing in on him. His jaw tightened and his gaze kept going to the exit as if he were searching for a way out.

I nudged his knee with mine under the table, leaving it pressed there like a silent anchor. A small smile popped up and deflated. Then, Max, ever intuitive, shifted at my feet. He pressed his small, wiry body against Caleb's legs. He let out a quiet huff, *"I'm here."*

Caleb's finger twitched, then sought out Max's head beneath the table. The tension in his shoulders eased. His breathing slowed, no longer sharp and shallow.

Good job, Max.

"I help."

I focused on Caleb's fingers running through Max's wiry hair, grounding him. And that seemed to ground me, too. Somewhere during Oliver's hilarious recounting of a burst pipe mishap, Caleb reached for my hand, intertwining his fingers with mine. My whole body sighed.

The betrayal from years ago lingered, a dull ache just beneath my breastbone. But sitting here, Caleb mostly relaxed at my side, laughing at Oliver's dramatic retelling of his home repairs gone wrong, I couldn't deny the warmth of the moment. The scents of grilled meat, hoppy beer and the faintest whiff of Aimee's jasmine perfume were a reminder of a friendship I'd once thought unshakable.

The night ended with the four of us, along with Max, spilling out into the cool night air. The autumn breeze was a welcome contrast to the heat of the crowded pub. Caleb let out a breath as if he'd been holding it for hours. Max instinctively kept himself between Caleb and everyone else, creating space.

"It was really nice to finally meet you, Lark. And you, too, Caleb." He extended a hand to each of us. "I've heard so much about both of you from Aimee." Oliver clapped Caleb on the back. "We should do this again soon."

Caleb nodded.

Aimee glanced at me, one arm around Oliver's waist, the other gripping her purse as if she feared someone would snatch it from her. "Goodnight, Lark."

I nodded, a short, stiff movement. "'Night."

As Aimee turned away, something in me wavered, a pull in my chest I couldn't name. The past still stood between us, thick and tangled. But as she and Oliver disappeared into the night, that soul-deep longing pressed against my ribs, refusing to be ignored.

THE EVENING with Aimee and Oliver seemed to have loosened something in Caleb. He seemed more at ease, more open. When he offered to help me paint the dog suites the next day, I took it as a good sign.

So here we were, cans of various colored paint he'd snagged from the store cracked open at our feet. The scent of fresh paint mingled with the odor of sawn wood. I opened the door to the first suite. The space would offer a cozy sleep area—big enough to hold a dog bed, a water bubbler and all the toys a dog wanted for a night away from home.

"You're sure you want each suite painted a different color?" Caleb asked from behind me. "Won't it make it look like a toddler's birthday party?"

I tossed him a smile over my shoulder. "Dogs just want to have fun."

He groaned and handed me a brush. "I thought they were colorblind?"

"They see color. Just in a more muted way than we do."

He scanned the cans at our feet. "What color first?"

"I like this mint green. Nice and restful."

He grabbed a paintbrush of his own, grazing my elbow. Just a brief pass in the narrow aisleway, but my skin prickled under my sweatshirt. I gave a silent shake. He was Liam's best friend. He'd practically lived at our house growing up, especially during the summers. I didn't want to make things difficult between them. And Liam needed his friend right now. More than I needed a complication.

Oblivious to my mental roller coaster, Caleb dipped it into the tangerine paint and swiped it across the wall of the second suite.

We'd worked for about twenty minutes when something overtook me. I dipped a thin paintbrush into a can of darker green paint. I crouched by the back wall and chuckled.

Caleb paused mid-stroke, watching me out of the corner of his eye. "You changing the design?"

I didn't look up. "Just adding a little something. For fun."

Squinting, he leaned closer. "Is that ... barking?"

I grinned and leaned back, showing off the neat line of painted script that read, "Woof, arf-arf, grr, ruff."

"Okay," he said, amusement glinting in his eyes. "What am I looking at?"

"I'm hiding motivational quotes for the dogs."

Caleb blinked. "In bark?"

"They wouldn't get verse." I tilted my head, then added a paw print period. "My mom used to write positive statements on the wall before she painted them. She said it made the room feel more alive and lighter."

"I remember." He chuckled. "That one summer she decided to paint Liam's room, she wrote, 'I choose to keep my room clean and orderly' in huge letters on the wall. Don't think it worked all that well."

I shrugged a shoulder. "I want the dogs to feel at home, you know. A little pick-me-up for when they're nervous or missing their people."

"You realize they can't read."

"It's not the words, it's the intent beneath the words they'll feel." I looked up from my next quote. "This one says, 'You are brave. Even when the big dogs bark.'"

He laughed, a low, easy sound that made my heart yearn something foolish. "That's honestly kind of great."

I smirked. "I figured no one wants to sleep under boring beige walls."

"Got another one?"

I didn't hesitate. I dipped my brush again and wrote, "Arf, woof, woof—grr, sniff."

Caleb leaned against the gateless doorway, watching me. "Translation?"

"You are not alone." My voice softened, almost as if I hadn't meant to say it out loud, as if the words hadn't been for whatever dog would sleep here, but for Caleb.

He didn't say anything right away. Just watched the words dancing across the wall.

I stood, rubbing my palm against the seam of my jeans, leaving a streak of green paint behind. "I know it's silly."

"It's kind of perfect."

Our gazes caught and held for a second too long. I made myself not read anything into it. Caleb took the brush from me. "Okay, my turn."

He crouched down, tongue pressed to the corner of his mouth and wrote in an unexpectedly neat script, "The journey of a thousand paw prints begins with a single sniff."

"Good one. Try more barking."

His forearm flexed as the paintbrush moved over the wall. A smear of tangerine paint decorated the edge of his jaw.

Mistake, I told myself, to notice things like that.

"Sniff, sniff, woof." Pride filled his voice.

I tilted my head. "Let me guess. 'Every day is a second chance to sniff something new.'"

He grinned. "Close. 'Believe in your bark.'"

I laughed, and when I did, something shifted between us—something soft and electric. He stood again, closer this time. Close enough that I could smell the cedar scent of his soap beneath the tang of paint.

"You always do that," he said.

"What?"

"Make ordinary things feel special."

I swallowed. My voice came out smaller than I meant. "I'm their voice."

"You are."

I looked up, paintbrush still in hand. "Woof, woof, ruff-ruff, yip."

Caleb leaned over my shoulder. "What's that one?"

"You are enough, even if you cry in your sleep."

He laughed again, the kind of laughter that made my cheeks warm, because the sound seemed to be just for me.

"Arf, woof-woof, sniff," he said.

"'You've got this even if you can't make it outside.'"

"Wrong." Caleb dipped his brush in the paint can again. "Love sometimes smells like bacon."

I choked on my laugh. "That's so Max!"

We stood back, gazes sweeping over the messy, half-finished suites—splashes of color, lines of nonsense barks that somehow meant everything. The kind of place a dog could feel safe. The kind of place that maybe would feel like home away from home.

Caleb shifted beside me, his arm brushing mine. He didn't step away.

"Can I tell you something?" His voice held a calm quiet.

I nodded, reaching for a rag to wipe the paint off my hands.

"This is the most fun I've had in a long time."

My heart tugged toward him. "Even more than when your brothers took you axe throwing when you first got home?"

"Way more." His gaze locked on mine. "There's no one I'd rather make weird dog art with."

Then before I could think or panic or pull away, he leaned in. Just slightly. Just enough.

I couldn't move. I couldn't breathe.

The kiss landed softly. No big moment. No dramatic swell of music. Just the sharp smell of wet paint, the faint scratch of denim against denim, and the press of his mouth against mine —warm and sure and entirely unexpected.

When we broke apart, my heart sprinted, my head swam.

"That was ..." I started.

Caleb smiled, a little dazed. "I think that was bark for 'Let's see where this goes.'"

I blinked, then grinned. "Ruff, ruff."

18

———

The Pumpkin Festival would open in two days. Even with working long into the night, I still needed to finish the story boards and stock the shelter's booth. I'd spent too much time finishing the dog suites with Caleb. Having fun when there was so much real work to do. We'd finished painting the suites, installed the rubber floor mats. Caleb built a sleep platform at the back of each suite, ready for beds. All that was missing were the doors.

"At this rate, we're never going to make it," I told the dogs as I handed out breakfast food bowls.

They didn't care. Food was food and they wanted theirs now.

I'd played phone tag with Caleb this morning. We were supposed to meet to install the doors and have dinner. Something I was looking much too forward to.

I poured kibble in Max's puzzle bowl. Not that it would slow him down. He pawed at my leg for me to hurry.

I placed Max's bowl in front of him. "With the Pumpkin Festival starting soon, he's probably busy at the store."

Max lifted his head mid-bite, beard speckled with kibble crumbs. "*My guy.*"

"Yes, your guy."

Rae appeared in the doorway, phone in hand. "Did you hear about the storm?"

"What storm?"

"They just upgraded the storm status. Possible tornado."

Tornadoes were rare in New Hampshire but not unheard of. Seventeen years ago, one had ripped through eleven communities, uprooting trees, flipping cars and tearing off roofs.

"Let's hope they're wrong." My gut churned. "We should still batten down the hatches, just in case."

Rae saluted. "Right, boss. I'll go tie down the outdoor equipment."

"Bring the smaller stuff inside. We'll stick it in one of the play areas."

"Aye, aye."

As she headed out, I grabbed flashlights and battery-operated lanterns. With the path projected to come close to the center later in the day, I called dog owners asking if they could pick up their dogs before the storm hit. Some could. Others were stuck at work. I filled every container I could find with water, double-checked the dog food supply, and distributed blankets in each suite.

I tried calling Caleb again.

Straight to voicemail.

With everyone buying supplies to ride out the storm, he was probably stuck at the store.

The storm barreled in mid-afternoon, the sky shifting from gunmetal gray to night black in seconds. The wind slammed against the building, howling like a mad beast. Rain followed—angry, insistent, pounding the windows and walls as if searching for a weak spot to break in.

Sadie and Bubbles pressed at my side on the couch, trembling. Max barked at the door as if that could chase the storm away. Hercules curled up in a comfy corner, blissfully asleep, while Fern, the toy poodle, found security in Rae's lap. Astro, a goldendoodle, clueless as ever, kept trying to shove a ball into my hand. Ranger, the shepherd, paced the common area like a sentry, stopping every few minutes to let out a growl.

The building creaked, making me hold my breath, hoping it stayed together. The air was heavy, electric. A gust of wind slammed into the building so hard, the wall behind me vibrated.

My phone buzzed. Caleb's name flashed on the screen. I answered, but the connection was bad.

"—damage—center—"

The call cut out.

I jumped up. "I need to get out to the new center."

Rae blocked my path. "No. You don't."

"What if—"

"And do what in the middle of a storm?" She grabbed my keys off the counter and backed up. "Whatever's happened, you can't do anything about right now. And the dogs need us here until the storm passes."

She was right, of course. But ...

Outside, the wind keened like a banshee. Something heavy crashed against the backside of the building. Sadie whimpered, pushing herself against my leg. I bent down, running a hand over her head. "It's okay, girl. We're safe. I promise."

Rae stared me down, wagging a warning finger at me. "Do not go out there at night."

The storm raged on. The wind. The rain.

The uncertainty.

I had to know. My future, the center's future was riding on that building.

"Can't make that promise."

~

ONCE THE STORM WEAKENED, I'd fully intended to drive to the new center, but as I gathered my bag and keys, my phone rang. "Is everything okay at the shelter, Phoebe?"

My only answer was a soul-deep sob. And that scared me because Phoebe was the strongest person I knew. Nothing unsettled her. "Phoebe?"

"Help me, Lark," Phoebe managed between sobs.

My heart thundered. This wasn't like Phoebe at all. "Where are you?"

Through her tears, she gave me an address. "It's bad. Really bad. The dogs—" She gulped in air. "They're in bad shape."

Phoebe was on rescue mission. Dogs were in danger. "I'll be right there. Dr. Ava?"

"Taking care of another emergency. Bring blankets. Hurry."

Getting to the house on the cul-de-sac took longer than I expected. The storm had left chaos in its wake—flooded roads, downed power lines sparking in the distance, branches strewn like discarded bones. My tires skidded in the mud as I wove around debris. By the time I reached the address, I had to look down twice at the map app on my phone to make sure I'd stopped at the right place, because only a pile of rubble stood there.

In the middle of the wreckage, the only thing I could make out was a blob of red. Phoebe crouched, pulling puppy after puppy out of the ruins.

"Oh, no." I grabbed a pile of blankets from my car and raced toward the ruins, rain pattering against my coat, wind blowing my hood off. Rain ran down my face like tears.

A makeshift kennel, on what looked like a back porch, had collapsed, the metal bars and wood sides were bent and twisted. Faint whimpers and desperate scrabbling sounds cut through the eerie whistle of the wind. The acrid scent of urine, feces and decay burned my nostrils. "What do we have?"

"A blasted puppy mill." Phoebe wiped the back of her hand across her eyes, leaving a streak of mud on her cheeks. "Over a dozen puppies. The owner just left the dogs there. Didn't even try to help them. One mom is gone." Her throat bobbed. "The other two are in bad shape."

She pointed at two French bulldogs lying on rubble, breath labored, skin folds crusted with dermatitis, ribs showing as if they hadn't eaten in a while. A pile of puppies squirmed, calling for their moms in scared mewls. One of the puppies nosed toward a mother who barely had the strength to lift her head.

I tucked blankets around the moms. For all the good that did in the rain. "We have to get them some vet care."

"As soon as possible." Phoebe pulled another puppy from a collapsed kennel, gagging. The stench was overwhelming. "I think that's the last one."

She sat back on her haunches, cradling the tiny pup in her arms. "The neighbor called the shelter. Said he'd complained about the guy to the police, but nothing was done about the situation."

"People like that should be made to live in those conditions. See how they like it."

"Hey!" came an indignant voice from the street.

I turned to see a short, bulky man dressed in jeans and flannel storming toward me, his face twisted in fury. Unlike his dogs, he didn't look as if he'd ever missed a meal.

"What do you think you're doing?"

"Rescuing these dogs." I picked up the sicker of the two moms and started toward my car.

Arms splayed out, the bully blocked my way with his bulk. "You're trespassing."

"You the owner?" Phoebe asked, tucking puppies into a blanket and snuggling them to her chest.

"Put those puppies down. They're mine."

"Not anymore." Phoebe marched toward her truck.

He lunged but wasn't fast enough. She stowed the pups in the cab and slammed the door shut. He grabbed her by the back of her red jacket and yanked her backward, hard. She stumbled but caught herself.

"If I were you, I'd drop me." Phoebe's warning came out ice-cold. "I've already called the sheriff's office, and the one thing you can count on is being slapped with animal endangerment charges."

"Mind your own business. It's not my fault the storm wrecked my house."

"It is your fault you kept those dogs in decrepit conditions." Phoebe glared at him over her shoulder, blocking his access to the blanket-wrapped puppies in the truck with her body. "I've photographed the horrid conditions of both the kennels and the dogs."

"You have no right to stick your nose in my business."

"We're taking them to the vet. You can see if the vet will let you have them back after the way you've treated them."

I rushed both moms in the back seat of my car. They both lay helpless as if resigned to their fates. Their snorts and snuffles sounded like cries. I tucked dry blankets around them to keep them warm. "You're safe now. We'll take good care of you and your babies. I'll be right back."

The man loomed over Phoebe, his mouth twisted. He raised a fist at her. My stomach lurched. I grabbed the heavy flashlight I kept under my seat. "Let her go. Now!"

He sneered. "Or what?"

I brandished the flashlight like a sword. "You lay a hand on her, and I swear I'll make sure the sheriff charges you with assault on top of the neglect."

Phoebe jerked her head back, knocking into the guy's face. Dropping his grip on Phoebe, he let out a garbled yell, blood spurting from his nose. He staggered backward and, before he could recover, we both rushed him. Phoebe kicked his knees out from under him, sending him sprawling in the mud. I didn't waste a second. I grabbed a slip lead from my pocket and hogtied him, jerking the knot tight.

Phoebe wiped mud from her hands on her jeans. "Let's go."

"You can't leave me here like this," he sputtered, writhing in the rain and mud.

"Why not?" Phoebe asked. "At least you're not lying in your own manure. That's more than what your dogs can say."

He swore. "You're going to pay for this."

Phoebe's phone rang and she answered it, her hands shaking. "Dr. Ava's going to meet us at the clinic."

I nodded and headed for the car. A weak, wheezing whimper from the back seat squeezed at my heart. I reached back, stroking the dog's frail body. "Hold on, girl. Just a little longer."

As we pulled away, the wind picked up, howling through the ruins of the house. I glanced in the rearview mirror. The man still thrashed in the mud, his shouts drowned by the storm's remnant.

The storm may be ebbing, but I had a feeling that, for these dogs, the fight was just starting.

19

———

By the time the puppies and their mothers were squared away, dawn broke in a kaleidoscope of colors —purple, candy-cotton pink, tangerine and baby blue. Today, the sky was calm, indifferent to the chaos yesterday's storm had created.

I left Dr. Ava's clinic with every bone in my body aching. The biggest relief was that all the rescued dogs should make a full recovery. Dr. Ava would do her best to make sure that none of the dogs were returned to the bully who'd abused them.

I needed a shower. I needed food. I needed sleep. But instead of going home, I headed toward the new center.

According to the news on the radio, a fifty-yard section of Quarry Road was hit with a micro-burst. Winds had clocked in at 95 mph. I had to drive around road and utility crews busy clearing the debris.

The entrance to Thistle Hill was blocked by two oaks, broken like toothpicks, lying across the road in a giant X that would take cranes to lift. I parked the car on the shoulder and got out. The air smelled raw—wet earth, split wood, and something electric that still clung to the atmosphere. The road was eerily still, like the setting of a dystopian novel. The distant growl of chainsaw and the occasional crack of branches replaced the usual chatter of morning birdsong.

Hope rose when the building came into view. The walls were still standing. The roof looked intact. Maybe it wasn't so bad. Maybe everything would be okay.

I fit the key in the lock and pushed open the door. A faint dampness infused the air, but the entryway was dry. The sawhorse, saw bench and saw were gone, leaving a clear path to the playrooms and kennel room. My hiking boots echoed on the vinyl floor, giving me the heebie-jeebies.

Then I stepped into the kennel room.

The smell hit me first—wet wood, mildew, and something metallic as if the earth had bled. At least an inch of dirty water covered the floor. Puffy white clouds scudded through a gaping hole in the ceiling, where shingles and plywood were peeled back like a wound. Wood, plaster, pink insulation had crashed into the sleep suites, turning them into a mangled mess. One of the suites had caved in, its metal gate bent like cheap wire.

My legs trembled, then gave out. Knees on the floor, water soaking through my jeans, I pressed a hand to my heart. A sob ripped from my throat.

This was too much. All of Caleb's hard work—crushed.

Ruined. All ruined.

A chime sounded from my pocket. My phone. I ignored it. I had ten days to relocate everything. Ten days to figure out where the dogs would go. How to run the Adopt-a-Thon this weekend ... How to—

A lump jammed my throat.

I looked around at the destruction, my vision swimming.

"So, you put in a sky light?" Aimee's bright voice broke through my despair.

My head snapped in her direction. She stood at the doorway, her tailored jacket too perfect for this mess. "What are you doing here?"

"I came to make sure the building survived the storm."

I lifted my arms. "As you can see, it didn't."

Aimee stepped inside. Water sloshed around her leather heels, but she kept coming. She crouched next to me and pulled me into a hug, ignoring the way her expensive trousers darkened with water.

For a second, I wanted to let go. Just cry. Just let someone else hold the weight for once.

But I couldn't. Not with her.

I shoved her arms away and pushed to my feet, water seeping off of me in a rush, turning my back on her. "I don't need you here."

Aimee sighed. "Like it or not you need a friend right now. And I'm the only one here."

"You're not a friend."

She let out a growl. "Lark—"

"Don't." I spun to face her, pulse pounding. "You don't get to stand there and act like you're some safe place to land. Not after what you did."

Guilt flickered across her face, but she didn't look away. "I know I hurt you."

"Hurt me?" I let out a hollow laugh. "You broke me, Aimee. You made me believe I could count on you, that you had my back—and then you shattered my life. You made me look like a fool for trusting you. You made me look like a fool, period." My throat tightened. "So, no, I don't need you now."

Aimee's mouth flattened. "You think I don't regret it?"

"I don't care if you regret it." My voice faltered. "Regret doesn't fix anything. Regret doesn't give me my life back." I waved my arms at the destruction. "Regret doesn't put this place back together." I sniffed back a fresh wave of tears. "Regret doesn't find my dogs a new home."

For the first time, something in her expression cracked. But then she straightened as if *she* needed walls. "Maybe not, but I can still help."

I shook my head, picking up pieces of ceiling and piling them in the center of the room. "Even with help ... it's too much. There's no point spending money to fix this place when it's scheduled for demolition in the spring."

Aimee was quiet for a long moment. "I'll find you some place."

I scoffed and snapped my fingers. "Right. Just like that?"

"Yes." She shook her wet trousers as if this was just another problem to solve. "I promise."

I wanted to tell her that I didn't believe her. That I couldn't believe her. Didn't dare believe her.

Because this wasn't just a business. It wasn't just a building.

The center and the dogs were my everything.

VOICES CAME from down the hallway where Aimee had just left. Who was she talking to now?

Then Caleb appeared at the door and my heart gave a warm flutter. But something was off. His gaze darted around the room, his fingers twitched at his sides. A thin layer of sweat glistened at his temples.

"I hope you didn't ride your bike here with all the mess on the roads."

"Are you okay?" As he stepped toward me, his forehead pleating, his gaze scanning my face as if he were checking for something broken.

"I don't know." Numbness spread through my limbs. My fingers barely responded when I flexed them. My legs were heavy, wooden. My thought turned sluggish. "All your hard work, it's ruined."

"We can rebuild."

I looked up at the ceiling with its gaping hole and let out a humorless laugh. "You make it sound simple." I gestured at the mess at our feet. "It's not. Not with my deadline."

"We can work through it." Something raw filled his voice, and I wasn't sure if he was talking about the ruined suites or his own PTSD.

Shaking my head, I swallowed the dam blocking my throat. "It's too much."

"What? You're going to give up just like that?" He folded his arms over his chest.

His words stung. Not because he was wrong, but because they were too close to the truth.

"I'm tired," I said on a weary sigh. So tired. "I've fought so hard for this place, for the dogs. And now?" I shook my head. "It's a pile of wreckage."

He took a step toward me. "That's not why you're ready to walk away."

My jaw clenched. "You've been gone for a decade. Don't pretend you know what's in my head."

"I know *you*." His voice softened. "You're scared."

I flinched. "I'm not—"

"You are." He tilted his head, studying me. "But it's not this mess." He gestured at the destruction. "It's something deeper."

I looked away. "Like what?"

"Like you thinking you've failed. But you haven't."

I had, though. The center would have to close, leaving all the daycare dogs in a lurch. The boarders who counted on a safe place while their owners traveled. If I'd taken Uncle Ansel's business advice, if I hadn't let my emotions rule my decisions, if I hadn't let fear ... "Maybe I don't want to talk about it."

"Maybe that's the problem."

A weight pressed against my chest. "You're one to talk."

"I can admit that I have problems. I'm letting you help me."

"Not without a fight. And you're not letting Max in."

He took another step closer. My fingers itched to reach for him. Instead, I wrapped my arms around my waist.

"When it comes to the dogs," he said, with such gentleness in his voice, "you always fight tooth and nail. You don't let anything stop you. Not bad weather. Not long nights. Not even people telling you it's impossible. What's different now?"

Tears burned my eyes. "It's too much all at once."

Caleb reached forward and twisted a stray strand of my hair around a finger, his touch soft, so soft. "You don't have to do this alone."

An echo of Aimee's words. "You say that like it's not something I haven't had to do."

His jaw tightened. "We can both try to change."

The silence between us stretched, heavy and charged.

He opened his arms. And with a sigh, I let myself lean into his warmth, his strength.

His arms wrapped around me, the scent of soap and cedar grounding me. Tears seeped, beading on the reflective material of his jacket.

Eventually, I pulled back and wiped my wet cheeks with the sleeve of my sweater. "Sorry about that."

"I'm not."

Before I could answer, a sharp crack split the air.

A weightless moment. A rush of cold air. Then—impact.

Something hard slammed into my skull. My knees buckled. The room spun. My vision dimmed, sound warping into an underwater hum.

"Lark!" Caleb's voice, sharp with panic. Hands, trembling hands, shook my shoulders. "Lark!"

Darkness oozed around the edges of my consciousness. Something slow and warm trickled down my temple.

"You're bleeding." His voice broke.

I tried to tell him I was okay, but my lips wouldn't move.

The world swayed. No, I was being lifted. Caleb's arms locked around me, his breathing ragged. Not from exertion, a part of me realized. From fear.

I'm okay, I tried to say.

He raced outside. "Aimee! Aimee! Wait!"

The sound of running feet. "What happened?"

"She got hit by a piece of ceiling. She's passed out."

No, I'm here. I'm fine. Just a little woozy.

"Let's get her to my car. An ambulance won't get here fast enough with all the road debris."

Jostling. Pain. My head pounded as if a jackhammer drilled inside my skull.

A car door swung open. The wind picked up, whipping my hair around my face.

"Put her on the seat," Aimee said.

Rustling. My body sinking into plush upholstery. *There's going to be blood on your fancy seat, Aimee.*

"Here," Aimee said. "Take this and put some pressure on the wound."

Caleb gulped. "So much blood."

"Scalp wounds bleed a lot. Get in!"

"No—I can't."

Silence.

Caleb, it's okay. You don't have to.

"You have to." Aimee snapped. "You need to hold that handkerchief in place."

Don't make him, I wanted to say, but my tongue refused to obey. *He can't.*

"I—"

"Get in!" Aimee ordered with a growl.

A sharp inhale. Then movement. The smell of sour sweat and spicy cedar mixed as he slid in beside me. His lap became my pillow. His hands, strong but shaking, pressed the fabric against my head. Not gently. Desperately.

The car jerked forward. Every bump on the road sent shards of fire through my skull.

Caleb's breathing—shallow, uneven. His pulse thudded where his hand pressed against my cheek.

It's okay, Caleb. I'm okay.

"Just hold on," he murmured. To me or to himself?

The highway blurred past. Then a screech. A stop.

"Get her inside," Aimee said. "I'll park."

Caleb scooped me up again and bolted toward the entrance that opened with a *swoosh*, like doors to some other world.

"Help!" he yelled. "I need help!"

"What happened?"

"She got hit with a piece of ceiling. She's bleeding."

Hands. Too many hands. The weightlessness of being passed between them.

"It's okay. We'll take care of her."

Movement. A new surface beneath me. A bed? A table?

"Now, go fill out the paperwork."

Caleb? My fingers reached out for him.

But he was gone.

And this time, when the blackness came, it stayed.

I woke up in a hospital bed, Mom and Dad sitting on either side of the bed. My mouth was summer sand dry. My head pulsed in a slow drumbeat. My nose filled with the acrid scent of disinfectant and weirdly, baby shampoo. "What happened?"

Mom reached for my hand, stroked my palm with her thumb. "You had a concussion, sweetheart."

Was that why my head hurt? I reached up, wincing at the gauze covering my tender temple. "When can I leave?"

"They're keeping you overnight for observation." Dad wagged a finger at me. "No arguing."

"The dogs—"

"Are being taken care of." Mom sent me a stern look. "You have to take care of yourself."

Deep lines grooved the side of her eyes. She was scared for me. Given that she couldn't help Liam the way she wanted to, I had to let her take care of me. I also needed to get out of here. I had too much to do to just lie there, doing nothing.

I shifted on the stiff bed. "Caleb?"

"He left."

"Is he okay?"

"I don't know, sweetheart. All that blood seemed to hit him hard."

I nodded and regretted it when pain swam through my skull. Aimee had seen him in a full PTSD episode. The heat of shame probably swamped him. Knowing him, he'd go into hiding. Would I ever hear from him again? Would I be able to convince him he needed Max?

"Aimee's in the waiting room," Mom said, a tentative note in her voice. "She's the one who got you here."

I couldn't deal with Aimee right now, so I said nothing.

"Paul, will you get me a cup of coffee?" Mom asked Dad.

Dad shifted in his chair, glancing at Mom. "Kate, maybe now isn't the best time. She's supposed to rest."

"What are you two talking about?" My voice came out a thin thread, but I was too drained to care.

"Take your time." Mom scooted her chair closer.

"Kate ..."

Mom smiled at Dad. "Thank you."

With a resigned sigh, Dad left. Mom took my hand again. "You and Aimee were friends, best friends—"

I braced for the coming argument. "You don't understand—"

"I do." Her voice had a quiet steeliness, the kind she used when she wasn't going to let something go. "She hurt you. She betrayed your trust. I know all that. But you were closer than sisters. And that kind of love just doesn't disappear."

My chest ached. I'd tried so hard to erase Aimee from my life, but a piece of me never did let her go. We did everything together as kids—sledding at Candlewick Park until our cheeks were numb, riding bikes around town from dawn to dusk, whispering secret hopes and dreams under the stars.

I forced myself to swallow. "I can't forgive her. I just can't."

"How does that feel?" Mom asked, voice quilt-soft, a gentle embrace.

The broken pieces of my heart bled again. "Like a wound that won't ever heal."

"Exactly." Mom sat up straighter and leaned in. "So, here's what we're going to do. I'm going to invite Aimee in—"

"No, Mom, please." My pulse pounded at my temples.

"—and we're going to hash this out. Together." She rubbed my fingers. "You won't be alone. I'll be right here, holding your hand."

My jaw tightened. "You don't get it. I can't just move past this because you want me to."

She sighed. "I talked to a friend who's a therapist, and she gave me some rules of engagement."

I let out a dry laugh. "You're making it sound like we're at war."

"Aren't you?" Her smile was meant to cushion the sting. "It takes two to break a friendship. And it takes two to repair it."

"I—"

"Life is short, Lark. You've already lost twelve years because of your stubbornness. You can't ever get those years back." She jostled my hand back and forth. "You have nothing to lose by hearing her out. And you have a friend to gain."

I sighed. She wouldn't let go. And I was too tired to fight. "So, these rules ..."

"While Aimee speaks, you will listen. No criticizing, no interrupting, no complaining. Once she's done talking, you'll have your turn."

I crossed my arms, the IV tugging at my skin. "What if I don't want a turn?"

Mom studied me, and I read disappointment in her eyes. "Then you don't take one. But at least you'll have heard her side."

I bit the inside of my cheek, searching for a way out. "What if she just wants to clear her conscience? What if it's all about making *her* feel better?"

Mom hesitated. "Maybe it is. Maybe it's also about healing something in you." She brushed away a stray strand of hair from my cheek. "I know you, sweetheart. You've missed her. And you don't let people in easily."

"That's not true," I mumbled.

The worst part was that I *had* missed her. Even now, every time something happened, my first thought was to call Aimee. Then I remembered what she'd done, and hurt all over again.

Mom tilted her head. "You love your dogs. I get the feeling you care for Caleb. But you haven't had a real friend in years. Not someone who knows you and cares for you the way she did."

I turned my gaze to the ceiling, staring at the rust-colored water stain on the acoustic tile. It reminded me of a peony in full bloom. "I just don't see how we can get past her betrayal."

Mom tucked the thin blanket around me, fussing. "Aimee regrets what happened, more than you know. We talked while the doctor was stitching your wound."

I blinked, caught off guard. "What?"

Mom took my hand once again. "She said she's tried reaching out, tried to apologize."

I closed my eyes tight. She still cared enough to keep trying? "An apology isn't enough."

"But it's a start."

My throat bobbed, working to stay ahead of tears. I was so tired. I just wanted to sleep. "Are you going to give her the rules of engagement, too?"

"Of course."

I let out a long breath. "Fine. But I'm not promising anything."

Mom smiled, rubbing my knuckles. "That's all I ask."

But as she stood to get Aimee, I wasn't sure I could go through with this.

WHILE MOM WAS GONE, fatigue weighed me down and, somehow, I drifted off to the rhythmic sounds of the machine monitoring my vital signs. When I woke up again, Aimee sat in the chair Mom had occupied.

"Hey," Aimee said, fingers knotted around a take-out coffee cup in her lap. Her smile faltered, then fell. She still wore yesterday's clothes. Mud streaks stained her jacket and water-marks soiled her slacks. Had she been there all night?

She pointed toward the take-out coffee on the table beside the bed. "I brought you coffee from the coffeeshop. It's better than the cafeteria one."

She reached into her purse and brought out packets of sugar and tiny tubs of cream. "I didn't know how you took it." She glanced at the cup. "Although, it's probably cold by now."

I hesitated, then reached for the cup. The cardboard sleeve was damp with a spill of coffee. I tried to peel open a cream container, but my fingers, clumsy and weak, wouldn't cooper-ate. Aimee took over, stirring in cream before handing back the cup.

I stared down at the pale cream, swirling into the black coffee. Did I trust her enough to drink this? Ridiculous. She wouldn't have done anything to it. Yet, the doubt lingered, bitter on my tongue. I took a sip anyway, expecting warmth, but getting a mouthful of room-temperature liquid that tasted like the pot's end. The harsh taste curled in my throat.

"Where's Mom?" My stomach gurgled. I put a hand over my belly. When was the last time I ate?

"She went to get you clean clothes. They're going to discharge you today."

"Good to know." I had so many things left to do on my to-do list for the Adopt-a-Thon. The Pumpkin Festival opened tonight, and this little concussion incident had put me way behind schedule.

Aimee stared at the coffeeshop's logo on the side of her cup as if it held the keys to this conversation. "I've missed you, Lark."

"So you've said." My voice was flat, distant—as if I were watching her from outside myself.

"I feel bad about how far off track our friendship has gone."

"I can't do this now." My fingers tightened against the coffee cup, its weight not solid enough to ground me. I glanced at the nurse's station through the door, a hive of activity, people buzzing as if they had someplace important to go. I envied them. "Mom was supposed to mediate."

Aimee swallowed and nodded. "I can come back."

"Let's just get this over with." I flipped my hand in a go-on motion.

"I-I value your friendship. I figured that out a minute too late. What I did was horribly wrong. It hurt you deeply."

That hurt rose up again, tightening my stomach, my chest, my throat. I forced my fingers to steady on the coffee cup's sides. "Did I do anything to make you feel like you had to strike out against me?"

"No!" Her eyes went wide and she shook her head.

"Then what happened?"

She bit down on her lower lip, the way she always did when she was nervous. "Remember when I spent that week at your place a couple of weeks before ... you know."

"You betrayed me?"

She nodded, twirling her coffee cup in her lap, shoulders curling inward.

We'd had such fun that week, pretending we were sisters. And that had made her betrayal sting that much more.

A sudden crackle of static from the intercom made Aimee jump. A voice called out on the intercom, "Attention! Code gray in triage! Attention! Code gray in triage!"

With Mom having worked at a hospital for years, I was familiar with the codes. Code gray meant violent patient. Were they anticipating what would go down between Aimee and me?

"Mom told me she was going on a business trip." She bit her lip again. "I should've known better. Secretaries don't usually go on business trips." Tears slid down her cheeks, and the cynical part of me wondered if they were real or crocodile. "She had voluntarily checked herself in at New Hampshire Hospital."

I gasped. The psychiatric hospital.

"Later, she told me she was in a dark place and needed help. She didn't want to burden me with her illness."

A monitor beeped an alarm at the nurse's station, the sound sharp and jarring. My stomach sank. Liam. Trying to save Mom from his pain by staying away. At least her mom had asked for help. "What does that have to do with what you did?"

"I thought I was protecting Mom."

"From what?"

"She was so fragile when she came back. I—I—" Her mouth flattened. "It hurt, Lark. It hurt to choose her over you. But I had no choice."

"I don't understand."

"I was afraid of ... what she'd do. I couldn't lose her. She was all I had."

Her father had left soon after Aimee was born, and her mother had raised her on her own.

Aimee let out a burst of breath. "They were going to out her."

They. The mean girls—Hannah and her gang of clones: Jessica, Samantha and Brittany.

I'd spent so many years believing Aimee had betrayed me

because she wanted to be popular. That she'd chosen social status over our friendship. She'd done it because of survival?

"I thought you wanted in with them," I said. "That's why you betrayed my secret."

"I tried to fit in, for Mom's sake, but I couldn't." She lifted her cup to her lips but didn't take a sip. Instead, she lowered it to her lap again. "What they did to you ..." She took a big gulp of air. "By then, it was too late. For Mom, too. They outed her anyway. And for you."

I was too hurt by Aimee's betrayal to care what else was going on around me. The whole town could've been on fire, and I wouldn't have noticed—that's how deep the hurt cut. I pretended I was sick for days. Mom eventually forced me to go back to school, back to the name-calling and the teasing and the ridicule. I wore it all like a concrete cape, pretending I didn't care. I arrived at school right at first bell. I spent my lunch time at the library and left as soon as the last bell rang. Spoke to no one.

She put a hand over her heart. "I'm truly sorry. I would like the chance to earn your trust again."

I stared at her, the weight of her secret settling deep into my bones. I had carried this pain for so long. Let it shape me. Let it carve away my ability to trust. But now ...

I rolled the cold coffee cup between my palms. The cream had settled, looking like mud. But I took another sip anyway.

"This is a lot," I finally said, voice rougher than I expected. "You're going to have to give me time."

"Of course."

I wasn't ready to forgive her. Not yet. But I guess Mom was right.

At least now I understood.

21

─────

I let Mom fuss over me. Let her tuck blankets around me on my couch. Let her make me chicken soup and peppermint tea and slices of sourdough bread spread thick with butter. Let her surround me with dogs—Bubbles at my feet, Sadie within arm's reach on the floor next to me, Hercules curled up on the chair next to the couch, and Max on my lap. Then I shooed her away with the excuse that I needed to rest.

"Call me if you need anything." She wrapped one more blanket around my legs, making me feel like a mummy. "I'll be back later with some dinner."

Food, the language of love in this family.

"Thanks, Mom."

I burrowed into the pillows, closed my eyes and petted Max.

"Okay, I'll leave you alone." Her footsteps neared again. "I'm putting your phone right in your pocket."

I smiled. "I'm okay. Like the doctor said, I just need to rest for a couple of days."

"You're right."

She left, closing the front door behind her. I cracked an eye open, watching her progress down my front walkway from the window. She got in her SUV, hesitated, then drove away. My phone buzzed.

Mom: Resting, right?

Me: Yep.

I ignored the twist of guilt. Not trusting that she wouldn't double back, I gave myself half an hour before getting up. The moment I did, the world tilted. I fell back on the couch, bracing myself until the dizziness passed. With slow movements, I pushed away the blankets. Max grumbled.

I reached for my phone and called Caleb. Straight to voicemail. I tapped the phone on the side of my hand, then called the store.

"Country Store," said a perky voice. "How may I direct your call?"

"Caleb Singer, please."

"Oh, I'm sorry, he's not in today."

"Do you know where he is?"

"Maybe at the festival?"

The Country Store did have a booth, but I didn't have high hopes of finding him there.

"Thanks."

I extricated myself from the pile of dogs. "Okay, guys. It's time to get you to the center so I can go check the booth at the festival."

"*I come!*" Max barked, front feet lifting off the ground.

Bubbles wagged her tail. "*Me, too.*"

Sadie hunkered down and whined. "*Stay!*"

Hercules snored on his chair.

I rounded up the reluctant dogs and drove to the canine center, hands tight on the steering wheel to stop another wave of dizziness.

Rae looked up from the computer and narrowed her gaze at me. "We're under strict orders to report to your mother if you show up here."

I lifted both eyebrows. "Does she pay your salary?"

"No, but she's intimidating."

I laughed. "That she is."

"You're not planning on working, are you?"

I tilted my head, regretting the move when a wave of pain swam through my skull. "Have you ever tried to sleep with a pile of dogs around you?"

"Um, no, but it sounds comfy and cozy."

I tutted. "It's not restful."

Rae took the dogs' leashes from me. "You're going back home?"

I nodded. *Eventually.*

At the fairgrounds, I headed straight for the shelter's booth, relieved to find it still standing. Wind had whipped through the open window, scattering brochures, knocking over displays and leaving a mess on the floor. Nothing compared to the hole in the ceiling and the water-logged wreckage at the old daycare.

I bent to pick up a clipboard and the motion sent a sharp throb through my skull. I gritted my teeth and kept going.

Outside, I rounded the booth and took in the broken fencing for the dog pens and the debris-strewn field beyond. So much for having the dogs there, luring possible adopters. So much for the agility demonstration and the puppy class.

Head hurting, I took in a deep breath. One thing at a time. I couldn't do anything about the fencing now. I called Aaron and left a message.

Phoebe stormed in. "What a mess! And the fencing! Did you see the fencing? We can't bring dogs into that mess. Too dangerous."

"Take a breath, Phoebe. I left Aaron a message. I'm almost done cleaning up."

Her forehead pleated. "Aren't you supposed to be home, recovering from a concussion?"

"Gossip never goes unshared in this town."

I still needed to get the adoption board with Aimee's photos and the dogs' stories up. I couldn't do that here, so I did have to go home.

Phoebe shooed me away. "I don't want to see you here tonight. I can handle the booth."

I lifted a hand in goodbye but didn't answer. I wanted—no, *needed*—to see the board go up, to see if people actually stopped to read the dogs' stories. If this was our only chance to get them adopted, I had to make it count.

My body had other ideas. A wave of exhaustion crashed over me, making my legs unsteady.

Phoebe grabbed my arm. "Whoa. You okay?"

I tried to shake off the heaviness swamping my body. "Yeah. I just need a minute."

She folded her arms and narrowed her gaze. "A minute home in bed, you mean."

I rubbed my forehead, feeling the steady pulse of a headache settling in. I should go home, go to bed and get a good night's sleep. But staying away meant trusting that Phoebe could tell the dogs' stories as well as the dogs could tell their own.

And after everything that had gone wrong today, I wasn't sure I could leave anything so big to chance.

"This dog," the man said, pointing at Max's photo on the board I'd put up an hour ago.

Festival lights twinkled. The merry-go-round music filled the air. The scent of pumpkin everything tempted fairgoers.

But no one else had even slowed down to look at the dogs on the board. Not even a second glance. No one had stopped with their own dogs to take a photo at the photo booth. But this man—tall and athletic, with a sharp focus that reminded me too much of Caleb—was studying Max as if he were the only dog on the board.

"What can you tell me about him?" he asked.

I hesitated. My grip tightened on the clipboard. Caleb should be the one asking questions and filling out the adoption forms, taking Max home.

I'd tried calling. Again, and again. Caleb needed Max as much as Max was certain he belonged with Caleb. I could see them hiking together, sleeping in that Adirondack chair, Caleb feeding him bits of bacon. Max wasn't looking for just any home—he was looking for *his* home.

And yet, Caleb was ignoring the bond they'd built. He wasn't answering my calls. He was turning his back on Max.

I forced my shoulders to relax. "He's a West Highland terrier. We think he's about 3 years old. He's potty trained and knows basic commands, but he can be a little stubborn. You'll want to take him to some obedience classes."

The man nodded, still studying the picture. Aimee had done a terrific job of capturing Max's personality—a little king of the hill, white against a bright blue sky. "Stubborn, huh?"

I gave a tight smile. "Determined."

He smiled back, a really nice smile. "I like determined."

I held my breath. The way he said it, so casually and confident, told me he wasn't put off by Max's "terrible" tendencies. He was still interested.

"He doesn't do well with kids," I said, hoping that would be a dealbreaker.

"That's okay. It's just me. I work from home, and I'd like some company." His gaze went back to Max's photo. "Do you think a little guy like that can keep up with me jogging?"

I imagined Max, ears perked, paws moving in quick, eager steps, ready and willing to go anywhere—but not with this man. With Caleb.

Max didn't belong with this stranger. He belonged at

Caleb's tiny home in the woods, lounging by the firepit. He belonged at Caleb's feet at the store. I could imagine Max saying, *you and me, we've got this*, when PTSD symptoms hit Caleb.

I forced myself to smile. "He has plenty of energy."

I willed my phone to ring. I willed Caleb to call.

But my phone stayed quiet.

"Can I see him?" the man asked, hope filling his voice.

"He'll be here tomorrow, along with some of the other dogs you see on this board." If the fencing was fixed.

An eddy of cold air swirled around my feet, dry leaves, tick-ticking against the booth's sides. I wanted to tell him Max wasn't just another dog. That the board didn't tell the whole story. That even though these were Max's words, there was more to him than his checkered history.

"Okay," he said, looking pleased. "I'll be back. Can you hold him for me?"

I handed him a clipboard, my fingers stiff on the metal clip. "Why don't you fill out the adoption paperwork, and we'll see how things go tomorrow?"

As he filled out the adoption questionnaire, unease pressed against my ribs. This wasn't just about Max. He was one of more than a dozen dogs that couldn't be here tonight because of the broken fencing. One of more than a dozen dogs who should be here, meeting people and finding a forever home.

The board wasn't working the way I'd expected. No one was stopping to read the stories.

Something had to change.

The man handed me the clipboard. "What's his favorite treat?"

I gave a wobbly smile. "Bacon."

"Smart dog." He took a snapshot of Max with his phone and gave me a nod. "See you tomorrow."

Phoebe strolled back to the booth, chewing through a giant burrito. "What are you still doing here?"

I pushed out a breath. "I'm leaving," I said, handing her the clipboard with the application for Max, my throat thickening around the words. "Someone's interested in Max."

"Yes!" Phoebe tucked the clipboard under her arm and wiped sauce off her chin. "If he qualifies, then we've got our first win."

I frowned. "It's not the right fit."

"We've been over this, Lark. This is about numbers. We need to get the shelter numbers down, or we're going to have to put dogs to sleep." She licked a stray bit of sauce from her thumb. "If this guy checks out, then Max is one step closer to getting adopted."

I gritted my teeth. "Finding the right home matters."

She sighed, exasperated. "Look, I'm with you. In a perfect world, we'd have the time to match the perfect dog with the perfect owner. But right now, we don't. It's about keeping dogs alive. We can't say no just because you don't feel like he's the right fit. Especially for Max."

This wasn't about feeling. It was about knowing.

Max *belonged* with Caleb.

I yanked my phone from my pocket and checked my messages. Still nothing.

Fine.

If Caleb wasn't going to answer, I'd make him.

I strode toward my car in the fairgrounds parking lot, phone in hand, thumb hovering over Caleb's name.

One more chance.

And if he didn't pick up ...

I'd go find him.

22

W hen I got to Caleb's tiny house, it stood dark. Only the flames of the fire in the firepit and the moon on the water lit the night. The scent of wood smoke wafted in the air, creating a cocoon of comfort by the lake's shore.

I made out Caleb's outline, sitting in his lone Adirondack chair, shoulders slumped, gaze fixed on the flames.

I strode toward him, the world tilting from side to side with each step. I needed to get home and rest so I could represent the dogs at their best tomorrow at the Pumpkin Festival. I shouldn't have to stop here and check on Caleb.

I stood next to the chair, hands on my hips. "Why aren't you returning my calls?"

"I've been busy."

"I can see that."

He glanced up at me, frowning. "Shouldn't you be home, recuperating?"

"What's going on?" I crouched next to the chair, closer than I'd intended. "Talk to me, please. I want to understand."

"There's nothing to understand."

Except for a whole inner landscape of pain. "Max needs you."

Caleb ground his teeth.

"He feels you're his mission."

"I thought you didn't talk to dogs anymore," Caleb said, hiking up an eyebrow.

"I lied. I didn't want to have to deal with anyone's judgment." Especially not his.

He waved a hand toward me. "There you go."

"There goes what?"

"I don't want anyone's judgment either."

About what had happened on the ride to the hospital? Except that it felt deeper than that. A soul-level wound. I let out a slow breath, lowered my knees to the ground and gripped the arm of his chair. "It's okay to hurt. It's okay to ask for help."

He threw another log on the fire. Hungry flames licked at the wood, making it burn bright yellow. "As long as it's other people and not you, right?"

I didn't know how to reach him. I didn't know what to say to make him open up. "Someone is interested in adopting Max."

"That's good."

"No, it isn't." I moved to face him, my knees touching the toe of his boots. "He wants only you."

Caleb's jaw tightened.

My fingers dug into Caleb's knees, my frustration bubbling over. "If this guy who wants Max returns him to the shelter, it will mean the end for him. Max won't get another chance."

Caleb's jaw worked as if he were chewing words before spitting them out. "I *can't* be responsible for anyone."

"Why not?" I was running out of patience. "When Max can give you so much."

He squeezed the back of his neck, shadows from the fire flickering across his face.

Something about the depth of his silence made my chest ache.

"I care about you, Caleb." The words came out in a rush. My fingers slid up until they found his hands. Rough calluses met my fingertips.

He pulled his hand away.

"Lark." His voice was quiet. A warning. "I'm fine."

Heat burned my face. "Sure, because hiding from the world is a great coping mechanism."

"You're really pouring on the pot/kettle stuff tonight."

A sudden wave of fatigue hit me, weighing my limbs. "Are you planning on going back to work?"

"None of this is your business."

"You're right. Why should I care if you're throwing away the people and dog who want you ..." I got up too fast. Dizziness flooded. I wobbled, throwing my arms out to catch my balance.

"Lark?" The rustle of him standing. Hands reaching for me.

I waved him off. "I'm fine."

I pulled away from him and headed for my car, each step rolling as if I were on a boat at sea.

He swiped my keys from my hand. "You're not driving."

"What?" I snorted. "You're going to drive me?"

Without a word, he turned and hurled the keys toward the trees. They landed somewhere in the darkness with a soft thud.

I gasped. "Did you just—?"

He shrugged, then pulled me back toward the fire. "Sit down before you fall over."

I refused.

"You're the one who showed up here," he said.

"You ignored me. What was I supposed to do?"

"I'm ignoring everyone."

The fire crackled and popped, sending fireflies of light into the sky.

"I care about you," I said once more. "I care what happens to you."

"Don't."

Some sort of war waged in his eyes. The silence stretched and burned.

I turned back toward my car. Without the keys, I wouldn't get far. But I'd get away from Caleb and the wall he was putting up against the world.

He muttered something under his breath, his footsteps coming up fast behind me.

"You're staying," he said, voice low and rough.

I closed my eyes, my pulse thumping at my temples. I was not looking forward to crawling through the undergrowth to find my blasted car keys. "You don't want me here, and I need to get back to those who do need and want my help."

When I opened my eyes, he looked wrecked. "Please, Lark. If something happened to you while you were driving home, I'd never forgive myself."

And he was already carrying a world of guilt. "Okay."

AFTER CALEB POURED water to douse the dying flames in the firepit, he led me back to his tiny house. Then he looked lost as if he wasn't quite sure what to do with me.

To give him something to focus on, I said, "I could use a cup of tea."

He nodded and headed toward the kitchen. He rummaged through a cupboard and brought out two boxes of tea. "Sleepy Time or peppermint?"

"Peppermint, please."

He took his time preparing two mugs of tea and a plate of chocolate chip cookies, then he sat down next to me on the couch. "Mom thinks she needs to keep feeding me."

I laughed. "It's your mom's language of love. Same as mine."

"Do you think all mothers are like that?" He took a cookie, but didn't eat it.

"Most want what's the best for their kids."

He nodded. Why was conversation so awkward with someone I'd known almost all of my life? "Are you going to the festival tomorrow?"

"No." He placed the cookie on the table.

I decided not to make a big deal out of his answer and just keep talking. "The storm destroyed the dog pens Aaron built. And there's all sorts of debris over the field where I was going to do the agility demonstration and hold a puppy class."

Even though I wasn't hungry, I took a cookie to keep my hands occupied and bit into it. "Don't tell my mom, but your mom's chocolate chip cookies are better."

He chuckled. "I understand self-preservation."

"Everything's ready for the big day tomorrow. We really need to adopt out all the dogs. But the dog board isn't working the way I expected."

"Dog board?"

"I made a big board, using photos of each dog and their stories in their own words. But people aren't stopping. They see the midway's bright lights, food and games, and walk right by. I really hope that Phoebe can clean up the field and Aaron fix the pens so we can have dogs there. People would stop for dogs."

"If you can't have them all, can you bring a few to get that draw?"

Why hadn't I thought of that? "That's a good idea. I have a portable pen. It could hold a few dogs."

I tick-tocked my head. "Puppies are favorites, but it's the older dogs that really need a home."

"So have a puppy to draw in people, then a couple of older dogs whose stories can pull at the heartstrings."

I smiled at him. "You're good at this."

"You sound surprised."

"No, just ..." I shrugged. "I'm not sure exactly what you do at the store."

"Part of my job is to run campaigns to get people into the store. Not just for the expected hardware, but also for the things they never knew they needed."

I yawned. "That makes sense."

I leaned back against the couch. Caleb pulled a knitted blanket in shades of green from the back of the couch and tucked it around my legs. My skin prickled under the warmth of the yarn. "Remember the summer we decided to sell frogs?"

He smiled and shook his head. "We thought people would keep them as pets like we did."

"Then that guy bought the whole bucket and said he hadn't eaten frog legs in a long time."

"And you burst into tears and wrestled him for the bucket of frogs."

"You bought them back."

He reached an arm over my shoulders and pulled me closer to him. His flannel shirt was soft under my cheek and smelled laundry fresh.

"I would've done anything to stop those tears."

I placed a hand over his heart, its beat pulsed against my palm—steady, grounding. "Liam wasn't happy that you paid more for them than the guy had."

"Liam was hoping to get himself a skateboard with his share of the profits."

"When you handed me that bucket of frogs as if it were a prize ..." I looked up at him. "And when you headed toward the creek to put the frogs back in the water, that's when I fell for you."

Something warm and tender swirled through his eyes, and that scared me. He'd been my hero that day. Not just a friend anymore, but someone who owned a piece of my heart. I didn't want to fall for him again. There was no point giving my heart to someone who didn't want it. That was asking for heartache. "That is until you and Liam started teasing me about hearing dogs."

He twirled a strand of my hair around a finger. My scalp tingled. "I fell for you the day Liam brought you over to my house the first time. You were this bright, shiny girl who was so at ease in her skin. You knew who you were and what you wanted. And I was this awkward kid trying to figure out who he was."

"You liked me?"

"Always," he whispered the word into my hair, sending a warm shiver down my spine.

My body settled closer into Caleb as if it knew exactly what it wanted. I tried to pull away, but Caleb's hand held me in place.

"After high school, you left." I hoped he didn't notice the tiny note of accusation in my voice.

"Still trying to figure out who I was."

Especially with two older brothers who picked apart all of his choices. I could empathize with the not-good-enough feeling trailing behind like a shadow. "And now?"

His heartbeat lub-dubbed beneath my hand. "I still don't know."

"You don't like the store?"

"It wasn't my dream."

"What was?"

He shook his head, sparking shards of warmth against the top of my head that were much too enjoyable. "I wanted to build something of my own."

I lifted my head from his shoulder and looked him in the eyes. "You still can."

A finger traced the side of my face, and I instinctively

leaned toward his touch. "You're the only person who ever believed in all of my crazy ideas."

"They weren't all crazy."

He leaned forward, his lips stopping just short of mine. The warmth of his breath sent a ripple of anticipation through me. I should have pulled back. I should have made a joke or changed the subject. Instead, I did something stupid—I closed the gap.

The moment his lips met mine, the world faded. The taste of peppermint from the tea lingered on his lips, mingling with something distinctively Caleb—something I had no business wanting. His mouth was warm, yielding, hungry. My body whispered *yes*, even as my brain shouted *no*.

Then a wave of dizziness overtook me, making me wobble. I blamed this whole lack of judgment on the concussion.

Then, *bang*, something crashed outside.

I jerked back, heart hammering against my ribs. Caleb tensed, his hand protecting me.

"What was that?" I whispered.

He pressed his forehead against mine for half a second before pulling away. "Probably Roxy."

"Roxy?"

"The raccoon who insists on knocking over my trash cans."

A rustling noise came from outside, followed by another thud.

Caleb groaned. "I should go scare her off before she makes a bigger mess. Somehow, she's figured out how to unlatch the raccoon-proof lock."

I forced a laugh, trying to steady my pulse. "That's romantic. Chasing off a raccoon."

He grinned, but heat lingered in his eyes. "Hold that thought." He mimicked holding a sword. "I'll fight that raccoon for you and be right back."

He stood, grabbed a flashlight from the shelf next to the

door. I curled my fingers into the knitted blanket, my heart still racing.

Outside, Caleb and the raccoon seemed to hold an argument. For a moment, I wondered if Roxy would win. I laughed, relaxing.

When he came back in, he took one look at me and said, "You need to rest."

My whole body sagged with disappointment. I patted the space next to me on the couch. "Just hold me for a minute."

The cushion dipped from his weight and his arm settled around my shoulders. "I've got you."

My eyes grew heavy. My body sighed against his. I thought of the dogs and all the help they needed. I thought of Caleb, of his kiss, of how dangerous it was to fall for him again.

I should push away, go home. Safer.

Instead, I let myself relax in his arms.

Later, I would regret letting myself be so unguarded.

23

———

When I woke up the next morning, Caleb was gone. Both relief and disappointment swirled through me. On the table next to the couch, he'd left a thermos, a mug, a plate with an English muffin spread with peanut butter—a favorite of mine when I was twelve. I smiled. He'd remembered.

He'd also left a note. And my car keys. "Gone to store."

I couldn't decide if that was good, or just another form of escape—this time from me. Either way, I didn't have time to worry about whether something existed or not between me and Caleb. I had to run to the canine center and check on things, then get to the Pumpkin Festival before it opened at 10.

Caleb would have to wait.

AT THE DOG shelter's booth at the festival, things had not improved. People walked by. Children wanted to pet the puppy, but parents dragged them along deeper into the festivities.

"This isn't working," I mumbled, watching people walking

by, carrying pumpkins and cotton candy and stuffed animals won at games.

"At this rate, we won't adopt out any dog," Phoebe said, gnawing on her already chewed up thumbnail.

She'd tried pulling people over. She'd tried bringing the puppy right into the pathway of fairgoers. She'd tried calling out all the wonderful auction basket contents like a carnival barker trying to get attention to a sideshow. But nothing had worked. It was as if the booth was invisible. "We've had another three dogs show up at the shelter because people lost their homes in the microburst. Not to mention the Frenchies and their pups when they're well enough to leave the vet's."

I'd added them to the adoption board this morning, making it look overcrowded.

"I'm going to go get something to eat." Phoebe growled. "I think better when I'm chewing. Want anything?"

I shook my head. "Thanks."

We'd already lost half a day with zero adoptions. I glanced into the pen at the mixed-breed puppy with big brown eyes, a golden coat and an infectious personality. "How could no one have snatched you up already?"

He batted at the metal bars of the pen with a paw and whined. I picked him up, snuggling him to my chest.

The puppy nuzzled my ear. "*Hungry.*"

"You're always hungry." I automatically went to my jeans pocket where I kept a baggie filled with treats and offered him a couple. After a bit of squirming, he fell asleep in my arms. I sat down on the selfie hay bales, hoping someone would want to pet him.

But the flow of traffic sought out the buzz and clank of games, the sweet and savory scents of apple cider donuts and corn dogs, the thrill of the Ferris wheel and merry-go-round.

I couldn't bear the thought that Phoebe would have to close the shelter. That these dogs would never find their forever homes. That ... yeah, I didn't want to think about what would become of the "unadoptable" dogs. I wish I could take them all in but, of course, I couldn't.

I petted the sleeping puppy. "I can't let that happen. I just can't."

The squeak of wheels brought my attention back to the midway. There, coming from the parking lot, was Caleb pulling a cart filled with PVC pipes and orange netting. I thought he'd keep going toward the store's booth, but instead, he stopped at mine.

"What's all that?" I switched the puppy from one arm to the other, looking at Caleb for signs of what, I wasn't sure.

He wore a sheepish expression. "I'd hoped to have it done before you got here but I had to put out a couple of fires at the store."

I raised an eyebrow in question.

"I'm going to fix your pens. Aaron's running around with enough chores to keep him busy till Christmas. So, I thought I'd take this one off his list." He chucked his chin in the direction of the cart. "It won't be as strong as what was there, but it should hold for the weekend and allow you to show off more dogs."

"Oh, wow." I placed a hand over my heart, suddenly spilling over with warmth. "I don't know what to say."

"Thank you is customary."

I smiled, feeling it go all the way to my eyes for the first time in a long time. "Thank you very much. I really appreciate you doing this when you have your own booth to run."

He shuddered. "Naw, I leave that to the kids."

Phoebe ambled back, chewing on a funnel cake bigger than her head. "Are you looking for a dog?"

I speared Caleb with a look. "He already has one—Max."

Phoebe lit up. "You adopted Max?"

"I have not." He jerked the cart's handle, yanking it toward the back of the booth where the 4x4 posts and wire fencing lay in a twisted mess.

"But he will because they belong together," I said loud enough for Caleb to hear.

"Okay," Phoebe said, chewing another bite of her sugar-and-cinnamon-dusted treat. "I don't know what's going on between you two, but you realize that Chris guy is coming by after work to take a look at Max. If the adoption papers aren't signed by then, I'll have to let him take Max."

"I'm working on it," I mumbled, handing her the puppy. He stretched out, trying to lick Phoebe's funnel cake. "Can you watch the booth? I'm going to lend Caleb a hand putting the pens back up so you can bring more dogs."

"Uh-huh." She bent her head at an awkward angle and took another bite of funnel cake. "Work your dog charm on that handsome devil."

I rolled my eyes at her, and she laughed.

At the pens, I stood, hands on hips, watching Caleb studying the debris. "What can I do to help?"

"Looks like most of the posts are still solid enough. That twisted metal has to go. Anywhere safe to pile it?"

I took a look around. A light breeze lifted and looped the debris still littering the field beyond the pens. I didn't want anyone accidentally running into the wire and breaking skin. "Behind the poop bag center."

He nodded, donned a pair of work gloves and got to work, each of his moves efficient and capable, flexing well-toned muscles through his green flannel shirt. The well-worn shirt had a hole at one elbow, showing well-tanned skin. I had the stupidest urge to touch it.

I shook my head, found a second pair of work gloves on the cart and joined him. Working together, we moved section after section of broken metal. His proximity seemed to bring out the clumsy in me. At one point, I lost my grip on a downed post, falling backward and right into Caleb's arms. He caught me, both hands cupping my hips, sending a zing of awareness through me. This close, his scent of cedar and sweat made me think of the kiss, which made my stomach flutter all over again. It took all I had not to turn in his arms and ask for another.

"Sorry." I glanced up. He was already looking at me, eyes dark whirlpools.

Neither of us spoke. The moment stretched, buzzing like a downed electric wire. Caleb cleared his throat, released me, leaving me feeling adrift. He reached for the post and hefted it onto the refuse pile like a Scot competing at a caber toss, breaking the spell between us.

"About last night—" I started, not sure where I was going with that comment or why I was bringing it up.

He launched another section of wire onto the pile. "I don't regret it."

"Me, either. I just wondered if ..."

He straightened, sweat glistening along his hairline, distracting me. "If what?"

"It could happen again." I said it so fast the words ran into each other.

One side of his mouth quirked up. "Could be arranged."

"I'd like that." Face burning, I turned back to the last section of wire, feeling his gaze on me. What was I doing? Neither of us were in the right place to start a relationship. He was still dealing with the remnants of his accident. And I was still trying to figure out how to fit in this world that didn't want me.

Before long, we were unrolling the orange webbing. I held it against the posts while Caleb secured it in place. Caleb fashioned gates from the PVC piping. While I held the gate, he fitted it over a pipe. He reached around me to adjust the latch for the gate. His breath brushed against my hair, making my scalp tingle.

Phoebe came around the side of the booth, carrying three cups of steaming apple cider. "Looks great!"

Now that I wasn't moving, the chill of the October air slipped under my jacket, making me wish Caleb would hold me again.

Caleb stood back and inspected his work. "Almost done."

A gust of wind blew a strand of hair into my eyes, making me blink. Caleb reached out and tucked it back into my now-loose braid, his fingers lingering on my nape long enough to make my pulse scurry.

He held my gaze for a second, then looked away. "You should be able to bring more dogs in now."

With shaking fingers, I took the cup Phoebe offered and drank it too fast, burning my tongue. "Can you stop by the center and pick up Bubbles? She's so sweet that she should be able to find a home." I glanced at Caleb. "And Max."

He wiped a sleeve over his sweating brow, ignoring my comment.

"We need Max here for that Chris guy anyway." Phoebe handed Caleb a cup. He hesitated before taking it.

As we sipped in silence, laughter from the festival drifted over, along with the distant sound of a hayride wagon rattling along the path. The bright noon sun shone down, making every metal surface sparkle.

I wrapped my hand around the warmth of the cup, staring at the mist curling from the surface, hoping it would give me the right words to reach Caleb. He needed Max as much as Max needed him.

He downed his cider in just a few gulps, then filled the cart with the remnants of his supplies. "Hope that helps with the adoptions."

"You could take care of Max's right now." I put lightness in my voice and still missed the mark.

"I can't. Not now." His gaze searched mine, as if weighing

what he wanted to say. "It's just ... I'm still trying to figure things out."

"I get it." And I did. But that didn't stop the ache in my chest —for him, for Max. "Except that later will be too late."

A gust of wind kicked up, sending a flurry of leaves skittering around our ankles. A flying strand of hay from the bales stuck to his flannel. Without thinking, I reached up and brushed it away. His hand caught mine before I could pull back all the way, his grip firm and warm. He spread my palm over his fast-beating heart.

"Lark ..." His voice was low and rough. Then he gave one shake of his head and released my hand. "I have to go."

I swallowed hard. "Sure. Just run away."

He turned to grab the cart's handle.

"It's Max's last chance for a forever home, Caleb."

He stiffened. Free fist clenched tight at his side. But he didn't look back.

The cart squeaked away, disappearing into the festival crowd.

Beside me, Phoebe knocked back the rest of her cider. "That is one stubborn man."

I stared at the place where Caleb had disappeared, my cider growing cold in my hands. "I know."

24

"Is everything okay?" Aimee's voice came from behind me, floating above the soft sounds of the fairgoers milling around Candlewick Park.

I stared at the spot where Caleb had disappeared and willed him to come back. "Everything's a mess."

Around us, the Pumpkin Festival was in full swing. The scent of cinnamon filled the crisp afternoon air, making me crave an apple cider donut—or three. Giggles and the occasional shriek echoed from the nearby corn maze. Tinny music piped out of the merry-go-round, blending with the steady hum of the crowd.

"What happened with Caleb?" Aimee asked. "It looked intense."

My jaw clenched. I didn't want to betray his secret pain. It wasn't Aimee's business. "He left."

"And you wanted him to stay?"

I turned to face Aimee, ready to tell her to mind her own business, but something soft and vulnerable in her eyes stopped me. She was dressed in jeans, fancy hiking boots and a red fleece jacket, her dark brown bob windblown, her cheeks pink from the cool air.

She almost looked like the Aimee I remembered. But I wasn't sure that girl had ever really existed, except in my imagination.

"I want him to adopt Max." Voice strained, I turned toward the parking lot where festival-goers bustled toward the game booths and the food stands. "They need each other."

"But he's afraid because of his PTSD."

"That about sums it up."

Aimee gestured toward the selfie hay bales, decorated with pumpkins and gourds. She sat and patted the space beside her. That seemed too intimate, like I was forgiving her, which I wasn't ready to do, so I leaned against the selfie sign that read, "Dog Kisses 5¢." The sign had seemed cute at the time, now I wasn't so sure. What if people were taking it literally? What if that was why they were keeping their distance? Another failure.

Nearby, a group of kids posed for pictures in front of the jack-o-lantern pyramid, their parents hurrying to snap photos before the kids raced toward the caramel apple stand with its scent of melted sugar and butter.

Aimee tapped her lower lip with a finger, eyes scrunched in concentration. "We need to find a way to show him that having Max would benefit him more than being alone."

I gritted my teeth, pulling back on my temper. "You think I haven't been trying? Since the moment he walked into my canine center looking for a dog, I've been trying."

Her gaze sharpened. "What made him change his mind?"

"I'm not sure." I glanced at Max's photo on the dog board. The one where Aimee had made him look like a king of the hill, capturing both his sweet side and his stubborn side. "I think maybe he fell for Max right away and maybe that scared him."

Aimee studied me and gave me a knowing smile. "I can see Max isn't the only one who fell for Caleb."

My spine stiffened. "Really? You're going there?"

Her smile widened. "You've always liked him."

I hiked my shoulder into an I-don't-care shrug. "What do you know?"

"He's always liked you, too."

A flash of something old and painful tightened my chest. Liam and Caleb, my two best friends after Aimee, joining the mean girls' taunts.

"Yeah." I scoffed. "That's why he joined the crowd to make me feel like a freak."

I'd hated Liam and Caleb back then, just as I'd hated Aimee. I didn't know why it had been easier to forgive Liam and Caleb than Aimee. Maybe because both had suffered losses, and Aimee had gone on to thrive, seemingly unaffected by what she'd done.

Aimee dropped her gaze, twirling a strand of hay from the bale. "I don't have an answer for that. Except that fear makes people do things they don't necessarily want to."

Self-protection. I knew a thing or two about that.

Silence settled between us, muffled by the distant sound of popcorn popping in huge kettles and the hollow *thunks* of kids tossing beanbags at scarecrow targets.

Aimee let go of the piece of the straw. "So, what are you going to do?"

"I don't know." I let out a slow breath. "The booth isn't attracting people to adopt dogs. The only dog that's drawn interest is the one dog that belongs to someone else."

"Max."

"Max." My gaze went back to the board. His gaze appeared focused on me as if he, too, were asking the question of why I couldn't manage the simple task of convincing Caleb. "And Max can't get adopted by anyone but Caleb."

"You need attention," Aimee said.

"For the dogs," I corrected. "And for the shelter."

Aimee stood up, brushing hay from her jeans. "How about TV?"

I blinked. "What?"

She pointed toward the parking lot. A WMUR van had parked near the entrance gates. A cameraman leaned against the side of the van, eating a giant piece of apple pie and talking to a woman holding a clipboard.

The news crew.

Aimee crossed her arms. "The van's here, which means someone's here doing interviews. You need to make it so you're one of them."

I swallowed hard. Except that Sabrina Sands from the *Tri-Town Tribune* had already insinuated that dogs, even dogs in need, weren't special enough to deserve coverage. That the only thing interesting about the dogs was the one thing I didn't want to talk about.

I felt a nudge against my leg. The puppy. "How did you get loose?"

I picked him up and cradled him in my arms. He wasn't whining, wasn't making a sound. Just lying there looking at me, his eyes steady and full of trust. Like he knew. Like he was waiting for me to do the right thing.

The wind picked up, rattling the corn husks tied to the selfie booth posts. My nerves crackled like dry leaves.

I had a decision to make. Help the dogs or help myself.

And when I came right down to it, they were one and the same.

I turned to Aimee. "Can you watch the booth for me for a bit?"

Her brow lifted. "What are you going to do?"

I took in a steadying breath. "I'm going to find that TV crew and insist they interview the dogs."

Her hand shot out, fingers curling like claws around my wrist. "Lark? I thought ... You're not going to ..."

I met her gaze. "I have to."

Her forehead pleated into deep folds. "Are you sure?"

"Absolutely not."

But I couldn't see a way around it if I wanted to bring the dogs the attention they deserved.

The puppy let out a quiet huff, bopping his wet nose against my cheek saying, *Go.*

The scent of kettle corn and cider swirled around me, the warmth of the festival pressed in. Laughter and music and the distant bark of a dog—sounds that felt too normal, too easy, for what I was about to do.

Puppy still in my arms, I squared my shoulders. Took a breath.

Then headed toward the TV crew.

25

Heart beating like a manic clock, I headed back toward the booth. I was going to do this. I was going to blow my whole existence open. Whining, the puppy licked my cheek. *"Don't cry. Don't cry."*

I kissed the top of his head. *I'm okay. It'll be okay.*

For the dogs, I hoped. This last-ditch effort had to work.

Or I'd ruined everything for nothing.

Aimee stood by the booth, eyes wide, body tense, wringing her hands. "How did it go?"

"We got an interview." I swallowed the ball of dread in my throat and scoured the parking lot for Phoebe's truck. "I just need Phoebe to get here with the dogs."

Aimee glanced at the fairgoers hurrying by and lowered her voice to a whisper. "So, you're going to do … it?"

"I have no choice."

She grabbed one of my hands and squeezed it hard. "That's the bravest thing I've ever heard."

"More like the most stupid." I took my hand back and shook blood back into my fingers. "I've most likely shot my career into a million pieces."

"I wish I'd been that strong back in high school." Her forehead ruched. "I wish I could tell you everything would be okay."

I gave her a watery smile. "I wish you could, too."

She gave my arm a squeeze. "I have to go back to my booth, but if you need anything, moral support, anything at all during the interview, just call."

And for a stupid second, I wished she'd hug me just like she used to do when we were kids. "Thanks."

With a sad tip of her head, she hiked back to her booth.

I went to the small metal pen by the selfie booth and placed the puppy down. He whined. *"Hold me."*

In a bit. I had to psyche myself up for the interview.

"I'm back!" Phoebe announced, her voice loudspeaker strident over the happy noises of the festival.

She was leading half a dozen dogs toward the booth like a general heading to battle.

"Perfect timing," I said, sticking both my hands into the back pockets of my jeans so she wouldn't see them shaking. "WMUR is coming over in a bit to interview us about the shelter, the silent auction and the Adopt-a-Thon."

"Fantastic!" She wrestled the three shelter dogs into one pen. "How'd you score that?"

I gave a mirthless laugh. "By selling my soul."

She raised an eyebrow. "Okay ..."

Max pulled Phoebe away from the second pen, dragging Bubbles and another mutt with him.

"My guy! Where's my guy?"

I crouched down and scratched his neck. *He's not coming.*

"Why? Why? Why?" Max barked, front feet lifting off the ground with each sound.

Phoebe managed to untangle Bubbles and the mutt and lead them into the second pen.

I don't know. I moved to Max's favorite spot behind his ear and scratched him there. *But there's another guy who wants to take you home.*

"*No!*"

No kids. Just you and him.

"*No!*"

He seems like a good guy.

Max snorted. "*Not my guy.*"

But better than going back to the shelter.

Max turned his back on me, ears pinned back, tail a stiff, unmoving rod. If dogs could pout, he was pouting like a champion.

"What's up with him?" Phoebe asked, double-checking the latch on the pen.

"I think he's looking for Caleb."

Phoebe clucked. "He didn't sign the papers?"

I shook my head, heart breaking a little more.

"Speak of the devil," Phoebe said, jutting her chin toward the fairground entrance.

I turned to follow her gaze. For a second, I thought Caleb was marching toward the booth, his sure strides meaning he wanted Max. But the leather jacket and pressed jeans tore apart the illusion. My heart sank. Chris was back for Max.

"Hey." Chris smiled, a nice, friendly smile on a nice, friendly face. His eyes sparkled with joy at the sight of Max, still ignoring me at my feet. "There's my little guy."

Max turned up his nose and refused to look at Chris.

Max! I warned him. *This is your last chance at a forever home. Behave.*

He growled. "*Not my guy!*"

I gritted my teeth. *Your guy doesn't want you.*

Just saying the words hurt.

Max stared at me, pain swirling in his eyes. Something about the way he looked at me, betrayed and desperate, hit me hard. *I know, I know*, I wanted to say. He wasn't just being stubborn. He wasn't just a picky dog. He knew.

Max *knew* where he belonged. And it wasn't with Chris.

"Can I hold him?" Chris asked, his voice as eager as a little kid's.

I smiled and offered him the leash. "Of course."

Chris squatted down at Max's level, let him sniff his hand and patted him before attempting to pick him up. He was doing all the right things. This is a good placement, I tried to convince myself. His background check was clean. He had space, time and enough funds to spoil Max silly.

Max turned on Chris, growling low and deep in his throat. "*Not my guy!*"

"Max!" I picked him up and forced him to look me in the eye. "That's enough."

He whined. "*Not my guy.*"

I know. But it's the best we can do for now.

Max glanced over at Chris, then went boneless in my arms.

For a brief moment, I thought he'd given in. I handed him to Chris. Maybe this would be all right. "He's just afraid right now. He's had a lot of changes in his short life and hasn't always been treated well."

"Hey, I'm sorry little guy. I promise to take good care of you."

Then—

Quick as a flash, Max twisted, his wiry muscles tensing like a coiled spring. His jaw snapped around Chris' hand, not hard enough to break skin but enough to shock. Chris yelped, stumbling back into the portable pen with the puppy, knocking it over. The metal thudded against the wooden side of the booth, sending the dogs in the back pens into a barking frenzy. The puppy in the knocked-over pen yipped and sprang out. Phoebe caught him on the fly. As Chris tried to regain his footing, Max's red leash tangled around one ankle.

Max didn't wait.

He launched himself out of Chris's arms, hitting the ground running, his leash snapping against the dirt as he bolted.

Straight into the crowd.

"Oh, shoot," Phoebe said, dumping the puppy in the pen with Bubbles.

Chris swore, cradling his hand.

Phoebe reached for his hand. "Let me look at that bite."

While Phoebe took care of Chris, I took off after Max.

The fairgrounds were a blur of color—bright banners flapping above booths, flags billowing in the breeze. The air smelled of buttered popcorn and fried dough, making my stomach roil. Somewhere in the distance, the local high school band played popular film soundtracks, trumpets shrill against the low murmur of hundreds of conversations.

Heart racing Formula-1 fast, I could barely track Max. His small frame, weaving between legs, under strollers, past food booths, moved like smoke.

Someone shouted. A startled yelp. Max barely missed knocking over a toddler holding a melting ice cream cone.

"Max!" I shouted, breath burning in my lungs.

If I lost him now, I might never get him back.

26

———

I spotted a flash of white scurrying under the fence at the edge of Candlewick Park. Max was aiming for the rock bridge over the span of water separating Candlewick Lake from Brighton Lake.

The little devil was going to Caleb's.

I ran as fast as I could, my breath coming sharp and ragged, head pounding with each step. Unlike Max, I couldn't exactly cut through yards and squirm under fences. I had to take the long way—to Lakeshore Drive, past houses with scarecrows and jack o' lanterns. My pulse pounded harder with every step.

By the time I got to Caleb's tiny house, my legs ached, my lungs burned. Max stood barking in front of Caleb's door, sides heaving like a blacksmith's bellows. *I'm here! Let me in!*

Either Caleb wasn't home or was ignoring Max, which made me want to bark as much as Max.

I stomped up onto the small landing and banged my fist against the door. "Open up!"

No answer.

"What's going on?" Caleb's voice came from behind me.

I spun around to face him, heart still racing. He rolled his bike at his side, reflective gear glowing under the fading daylight.

Max bounded over to him, dancing at his feet, whimpering, licking his hand—so full of blind devotion that it made my throat tighten. Caleb barely looked at him. His jaw worked like a piston.

I closed the space between us and jabbed a finger in his chest. "This is all your fault."

His gaze snapped to mine, eyes stormy. "My fault?"

"Max ran away from his only chance at an adoption."

"How is that my fault?"

"You're being so selfish. This dog is going to miss out of a forever home because of your stubbornness."

He carefully leaned his bike against the side of the house. His fingers flexed and unflexed on the handlebars as if he were trying to hold something back. "I'm being honest. I can't take responsibility for anyone."

His gaze, sharp as a saw, locked onto mine. *Even you.*

The wind shifted, colder than before, rustling through the trees around us. I shivered but didn't back down. "What are you waiting for?"

He took off his helmet but didn't answer.

"Here's a newsflash. Nobody can rescue you." The words scraped along my throat as if they were clawing to get free. I was close enough to see pain wavering in his tired eyes, the war waging somewhere deep inside. He was running. Always running. And I was tired of chasing him.

Max barked. "*My guy!*"

"I'm not looking for a rescue." Voice flat, Caleb hung his helmet on the bike's handlebar.

I scooped up Max into my arms, his small body trembling, his heart a frantic tick against my ribs. "And yet, Max, with his big heart, is offering you that rescue. But he can't do it alone. You have to meet him halfway."

"*I help you.*" Max woofed.

Caleb swallowed hard, and for one second, I thought he might waver. His fingers twitched at his side as if he wanted to reach for Max, to take back his words.

But then he shut down. His eyes went distant, his jaw locked. "I'd like you to leave now. And take the dog with you."

The wind scraped leaves along the yard in a restless *ticktick-tick*.

"What happened?" I asked, voice raw. "What was so bad that you're turning away a chance at healing?"

His shoulders tensed. "Leave."

The word was steel, hewn from between gritted teeth.

Hugging Max closer, I blinked back against the sting in my eyes.

Max squirmed in my arms, whining, straining toward Caleb with every fiber of his tiny, stubborn body. "*My guy!*"

I took his little face in one hand and forced him to look into my eyes. I let him see my tears, feel my broken heart. "Your guy. Doesn't. Want. You."

Max let out a long, shuddering whine. "*My guy?*"

It's him, Max. Not you. You're perfect just the way you are.

But it was too late. My harsh words had found their mark and wounded. His little body went boneless in my arms, all the fight drained out of him. I carried him all the way back to the fairgrounds to the shelter's booth. When I placed him down in a pen, he didn't scramble to the gate, demanding to be let out. He slunk to the farthest corner, curled into a donut and tucked his nose beneath his paws.

I reached into my jacket pocket, fingers brushing against something soft. Max's favorite dragon toy. I stared down at it, throat closing.

I couldn't afford another dog, but I wouldn't let Max go back to that shelter.

Ever.

THE WMUR REPORTER showed up just as the sun bled into the horizon and the carnival lights popped on. She wore a navy fleece jacket emblazoned with the WMUR logo. Her long brown hair rustled softly with the breeze as if she were in a shampoo commercial.

I'd told Phoebe that the reporter would stop by but not why. She'd brought four more dogs to put a face on the situation. Hopefully, ruining my own life would help the dogs.

"We're at the Brighton Village Pumpkin Festival," the reporter said, bright smile for the camera, Phoebe and I on her right side at the back of the booth where the pens stood. We'd been fitted with microphones whose wire itched along my spine. The dogs, curious, all crowded around the gates, tails wagging. The camera rolling gathered a crowd.

"We're talking with Phoebe Flowers," the reporter continued, "who manages the Tri-Town Dog Shelter in Stoneley, and with Lark Eamon who runs the Stoneley Canine Center."

I did what I always did when I had to deal with the public, I put on a wide smile and an air of everything's-okay, when in reality my insides whirled as if in a blender set on high. I was surprised the microphone didn't pick up the hard beat of my heart. *It's not too late to back down*, the self-preserving side of me argued.

Then I caught the gaze of a gray mutt peering up at me, so trusting. I couldn't let the dogs down.

The reporter asked a few questions about each of our programs, then she got a gleam in her eye. "Lark, I hear that you can communicate with dogs. That you actually hear their thoughts."

Cue the skeptic music.

A rush of heat flooded my cheeks, my hands clenched tight.

Somewhere in the crowd, someone gave an incredulous snort. *Here we go.*

I swallowed against my dry throat and forced a no-big-deal shrug. "It's a gift I've had since I was six."

A brief pause. The reporter's brow lifted just enough for me to recognize the hesitation, the doubt. She wasn't mocking me outright, but she was assessing. *Is she crazy or is this a story?* "So ... how does it work?"

"It started when I was six and came across an abandoned dog. As I petted her, her voice rang clear in my head. At first, I thought it wasn't real, that I was making it up, but over the years, I've learned to trust the impressions that come to me."

In my peripheral vision, I caught a woman shaking her head, muttering something to her companion. *Loser. Weirdo. Liar.* Nails pressing into my palm, I braced myself.

"So, is it like whole sentences?" the reporter pressed.

"Sometimes. Sometimes it's a feeling. Or a knowing. Especially when it comes to placing the right dog with the right person." *There, my secret's out. Let's see how bad the fallout will be.*

The reporter didn't scoff. Didn't smirk. Her gaze held genuine interest. "Tell me more."

I exhaled too fast. "I just knew that first dog belonged with my grandmother. And she did. That little mutt made my grandmother's last years a joy. I knew another discarded dog belonged with my aunt. She didn't want him, but she ended up loving him with all her heart."

The reporter stepped closer to one of the pens and pointed at corgi mix, sniff-sniffing in her direction. "What is he thinking right now?"

I swallowed, trying to focus on the dog through my dizziness. "He's curious about your microphone. And he'd like a taste of that granola bar in your pocket."

She blinked. Her hand flew to her pocket, producing a bar

she'd clearly forgotten about. "Oh, well." She laughed. "It has chocolate chips. That's probably not good for him."

"I wouldn't recommend it." I took a small bone-shaped treat from my pocket. "But give him this and he'll be your friend forever."

She offered him the treat. He gobbled it down, then stared at her for more.

"He'd like to go home with you," I said.

She grinned but shook her head. "I don't think my two dogs would welcome a third."

"That's too bad." I rushed through my talking points, hoping to get them all in before she called the interview to an end. "We have fifteen dogs in dire need of finding a home. The shelter's overcrowded and the funds just aren't there to maintain the upkeep on all these dogs. Not to mention the space. Would you like to see our auction baskets? These will help keep the shelter open through the winter, so be generous when you place your bids."

She had the cameraman pan over the tables of baskets and placed a bid on several of the items. Then, she turned back to me. "Dogs are creatures with a generous spirit. I know mine offer me unconditional love when I need it most."

The camera zoomed in on the dogs in the pens again, capturing their eager faces.

Then out of nowhere, Aimee pushed through the crowd.

"That black-and-white dog?" She pointed to Bubbles. "Would she like to come home with me?"

I hesitated. Bubbles was special. She needed someone just as special. Would Aimee devote enough time and care to her?

Bubbles twirled in a happy circle. "*Yes!*"

"Yes." I barely got the words past my lips. "She says yes. She likes the way you smell."

Aimee gave a breathless laugh as if she hadn't been sure of Bubbles' answer. "What's the procedure to adopt her?"

I reached for a clipboard with an adoption form. My hand trembled, but my voice stayed smooth. "Fill that out, and she can go home with you tonight."

Aimee reached over the pen and scrubbed both sides of Bubbles' neck. Bubbles rewarded her with a happy lick across her cheek.

Then the crowd seemed to come alive.

A second person hesitated, glancing at me, gaze alive with questions. "What about him?"

Another. "Would this one like to come home with us?"

A floodgate burst open.

I was surrounded—voices overlapping, hands pointing, questions flying at me. The space that had once felt open now pressed in. A child tugged at his mother's sleeve, begging to bring home the last puppy.

A man nodded at the Lab mix. "I always wanted a dog like this. What does he think, Lark?"

Phoebe had to make another trip to the shelter. Dogs were placed. Forever homes were found. Families were made. And by the end of the evening, only three dogs remained, including Max still curled up in a corner of the pen.

I should have felt victorious. I should have felt triumphant.

Instead, I felt strangely drained.

As the last family left, doggie gift bag in hand, Phoebe cornered me. Her dark curls writhing around her head like angry asps, eyes flashing. "How could you blindside me like this?"

27

Phoebe's face contorted into a mask of pain. "I thought we were friends."

With the sun having set over the fairgrounds, the temperature plummeted, and the breeze wove icy fingers through the weave of my jacket. I rubbed my arms, hoping for some warmth and shivered instead. "We are."

Phoebe took a step back, fists pumping at her sides with every word. "Then *why* didn't you tell me?"

"Because I wanted us to stay friends." My voice wavered. I hadn't wanted her to stop me—for any reason. She'd made such a point that saving the dogs, getting them adopted was the most important task of this Adopt-a-Thon. I'd needed her to stand beside me, to do the interview. I hadn't really thought past that. Of the consequences.

"This lack of trust is making it hard for me to even think of you as a friend." She almost spit out the words.

A wave of sadness swamped through me, thick and suffocating. I swallowed against it, but my throat stayed tight. "You have to understand. The usual reaction when I tell people I can talk with dogs is not positive. There wasn't enough time to explain."

Her arms went wide out to her sides, encompassing the whole park. "If you thought knowing you can talk with dogs would destroy our friendship, then how could you tell the whole world on television?"

"For the dogs." Everything I did was for the dogs. My gaze went to Max, still curled up in the pen. Near him, Daisy and Duke, a bonded pair of beagle-mix mutts, watched us, ears pinned back. Daisy whimpered and tucked her tail. Duke growled low in his throat, a deep bass sound, and edged closer to Daisy.

Phoebe's voice dropped to a whisper, raw and filled with something that sounded like loss. "I feel betrayed."

Like I'd felt after what Aimee had done to me in high school. That familiar bitter ache spread through my chest. And even realizing the words were not enough, would never be enough, I said, "I'm sorry."

She jammed her hands into the windblown mess of her curls and pulled back. "What if this hurts the shelter?"

"It's helped adopt twelve dogs."

Phoebe's phone buzzed and buzzed again. She glanced at the screen. Her face tightened. "Your stunt might cost us. That was Jethro from the Feed & Seed. He's worried about our partnership."

Her phone buzzed again. She jabbed her finger at the screen. "And here's Annie from the insurance company, asking for an explanation."

A chill went down my spine. "I—"

But what could I say? I hadn't thought about how far the consequences might ripple. Just about saving the dogs.

She shook her head. "Why didn't you discuss this with me? We could've come up with a plan. Done this in a way that wouldn't hurt the shelter."

"There wasn't enough time. I had to make a split-second decision." I raked in a mountain of air. "You don't understand how hard it was to say out loud what I said, how much it took out of me, knowing that it would ruin my career."

"*Pfft.*" Her hands moved forward and out as if she were pushing me away. "Your career?"

"Who's going to want a trainer that speaks with dogs?"

She let out a bitter laugh. "Probably everyone who loves their dog and wants to understand them."

"You think I did this for my own profit? Did you not hear the sneers in the crowd?" I pointed in the direction where the crowd had stood only a few hours ago. "That's what I had to deal with growing up. Being called names. Being snubbed."

"But you're a grown woman now." Her mouth twisted and she lifted her hands in a what-gives motion. "That skill is something a lot of people would kill for. Look at how many dogs found the right family because you could ask them if they wanted to go home with those humans."

I hugged myself tighter. "Do you realize that you're the first person who's wanted to be my friend in over twelve years?"

I'd been alone, so alone. I hadn't realized how alone. I didn't know the rules anymore.

For a moment, her face softened, and I thought things would be okay. But she straightened, body stiff. "And you couldn't trust me?"

"I couldn't trust anybody." The words came out on a whisper.

"I feel sorry for you, then." She turned away, grabbing leashes and clipboards and shoving them into the supply bin with jerky movements, then jamming the box inside the booth and slamming the door. As she pulled the pen gate open, the latch clanked. She stepped inside.

Daisy slunk toward her, head low as if she expected a slap, Duke right behind her. Daisy pawed at Phoebe's leg and let out a low whine. Phoebe reached down to pat the dog's head. "It's going to be okay."

But her voice, the motion of her hand on Daisy's head were distracted, her mind already miles away.

"I'm taking the dogs back to the shelter." Her voice was flat.

"Not Max. He's mine."

She gave a sharp nod and attached a leash to both dogs' collars. As she walked by, she didn't even look at me.

Something inside me cracked. The cold didn't just nip at my skin, it seeped into my bones, hollowing me out. In the distance, the fairground lights popped off, one by one. The space between Phoebe and me became impossibly dark.

I wanted to erase this conversation. I wanted to go back to this morning. I wanted to trust her with my fears.

But it was too late.

Once again, I'd tried being myself.

Once again, it wasn't enough.

I DROPPED Max off at the center and made him comfortable in his suite with his favorite fleece blanket. He turned his back on me, refusing to eat, and ignoring his favorite stuffed dragon. When I went to pet him goodbye, his skin rippled as if he could shake off my touch.

Wiping the tears from my eyes with the back of my hand, I let him be. Gaining back his trust would take time. Tomorrow, I would fill out the adoption paperwork and he would never again have to worry about returning to the shelter. It was the least I could do.

Before I could do that, I had another stop to make. And this one would be just as hard.

I gathered Bubbles' pink blanket, her favorite rubber ball and her favorite fish-shaped chew toy and put them in a bag. I drove out to Thorned Bough, then sat in the car for a long time, mesmerized by the warm yellow light spilling from the windows, so cheerful and homey.

Heart knocking against my ribs, I grabbed the bag and headed to the door. I had no idea what I was going to say.

Oliver answered my knock, a smile lighting up his face when he recognized me. "Hi, Lark. How can I help you?"

"Is Aimee home?" I held the bag's handle tight in front of me with both hands.

He stepped aside, holding the door open. "I'll go get her."

She came down the stairs, Bubbles at her side. When Bubbles saw me, her tail went wild, and she nearly tripped down the stairs in her excitement.

Laughing, Aimee steadied her. "Easy, girl."

Bubbles bounded toward me, licking my hand and whining. I crouched beside her and ran my fingers through her silky coat, my throat tightening at her joy.

Are you happy? I asked her.

She barked. *"Play. Run. Eat."*

I'm glad.

"Hey, Bubs!" Oliver said. Bubbles' head snapped toward him, adoration in her eyes. "Want to go make the rounds with me?"

She barked and danced to Oliver's side.

Oliver wrapped an arm around Aimee's shoulders and kissed the top of her head. "I'll be back in a bit."

Man and dog left in a happy tangle of laughter and barks.

Aimee watched them from the window, a soft smile curving her lips. "Yeah, I think she's going to be Ollie's dog. She follows him like a shadow, always so happy to see him."

"I'm glad." I wasn't sure what to say, what to do. "She's happy."

Aimee turned toward me, fingers smoothing the seams of

her gray lounge pants before gesturing toward the living room. "Come in."

I followed her to the couch, inviting with all its soft earth-toned pillows, but couldn't make myself sit.

She hesitated, and stayed standing, too. "Is everything okay?"

My attempt at a smile felt like a grimace. I shook my head. "I just wanted to check on Bubbles. And to say ... thank you. For being the first person to adopt this afternoon. After the interview. But if you don't really want a dog, I'll take her back."

She made a dismissive noise, shaking her head. "I fell in love with her the first time you came over. I was worried about not being able to spend enough time with her and how that wouldn't be fair. That's why I didn't adopt her on the spot." Her eyes softened. "Looks like I don't have to worry about that. She adores Oliver, and he works from the barn, so it's perfect. Lara also said I could bring her to work if I want."

I tipped my head, weighing her words. "You really want her?"

"Absolutely." She glanced out the window where Oliver and Bubbles' shadows twined and twirled on the ground at the vineyard's edge. "She's extraordinary. Her one missing leg doesn't stop her at all."

"No, it doesn't." I hesitated. "It does require special care, though."

"I've already left a message with Dr. Ava."

I shoved the bag I held toward her. "I brought her favorites, just in case."

Aimee peeked inside the bag. "Thank you." She laughed, a small, real sound. "I think Oliver's already put Chewy out of business with everything he's ordered for her."

Bubbles would have a good life here. I was happy for her. "Just an FYI, with that long coat, I wouldn't let her sleep in your bed."

Aimee frowned.

"Ticks," I said. "You're out in the country where there's a lot of grass. You don't want to get Lyme because a tick migrated from her coat to your sheets."

She shivered. "I'll keep that in mind."

Silence settled between us, thick and awkward. The air felt too still, yet too charged. As if we were both waiting for something.

"We're planning on signing up for classes," Aimee said.

"There might not be a center for much longer."

"Private classes?"

But my mind was too filled with losses to think that far into the future.

"I—" I started, then stopped, rolling my lips inward. I stared at my hiking boots, crusted with mud from the fairgrounds, suddenly worried I'd tracked dirt all over Aimee's polished floor.

"What is it?" Aimee's voice was quiet.

I swallowed hard. "I wanted to apologize."

Her breath caught.

"For not allowing you to explain all those years ago." Phoebe had mirrored to me just how awful it was to be shut out.

Aimee's throat worked and she gave a nod. "I understand."

I licked my dry lips and let my gaze meet hers. "I would have picked my mother, too."

She sucked in a breath.

My hand went to my heart. "A child has a special tie with her mother." They'd shared the same heartbeat for months. "I'm sorry I couldn't hear your pain then."

Aimee's eyes shimmered. Her voice cracked. "You were too filled with your own."

Still clutching the bag, she stepped forward, her movement hesitant at first. Then she pulled me into a hug.

For a second, I stiffened. Then something inside me broke, and I melted into her arms.

Her hug was warm. Familiar.

"I'm sorry, too," she whispered.

Tears burned my eyes. I squeezed them shut, my face pressed against Aimee's shoulder, the scent of her jasmine fragrance soothing me. Her hand rubbed slow circles against my back—like she used to do when we were kids.

A sob broke free.

For the first time in years, I let myself lean into her.

And she held on.

28

The next morning, I woke up alone in my bed. Alone in my house. Completely alone. Sadie and Hercules had spent the night at the center, along with Max.

I sat up and swung my legs over the side of the bed, toes curling against the cold wooden floor. Aimee had lived at Thorned Bough for about six weeks and her house already felt like a well-lived, well-loved home. Hers.

I looked around at the bedroom that had once belonged to my grandmother. Her dresser, her sleigh bed, her night table with her faux-Tiffany lamp, her pale lavender walls. I'd lived here for over a decade, and it still felt like my grandmother's house. The air was as stale as an old trunk that had remained closed too long.

"You can do something about it." And suddenly, the thought of painting the bedroom walls a restful green or blue elevated my mood. Paint didn't cost much, and it would change the whole atmosphere of the house. Make it more mine.

Plan forming, I made coffee, took the time to pour it into a ceramic mug instead of my usual travel mug and sat at the round kitchen table, watching the squirrels bury acorns all over the back yard while eating my English muffin.

The near-constant dinging on incoming texts grated on my nerves. I ignored them and focused on trying to find peace with all that had happened over the past few days. Like Max, part of me wanted to curl up and sleep until this whole mess had passed over. Except that I did have to go to the center and check up on the dogs, on Max, and make sure he was okay.

And I did have to face the consequences of what I'd done.

Which meant going back to the fairgrounds for this last day of the Pumpkin Festival.

When I got to the center, Phoebe was waiting, arms a fortress around her, foot tapping impatiently on the linoleum. Her face was unreadable, but her rigid stance said enough.

"You started this mess," she all but hissed. "You get your butt to the fairgrounds and finish it."

Before I could say anything, she brushed by me, knocking my shoulder hard enough that I had to take a step back to steady myself.

Rae gave me a look. "What was that about?"

"You haven't watched the news?"

"Who does?"

Apparently not Gen Zers. Head bent over her screen, her thumb scrolled through her phone. Her eyes went wide. Her head snapped up, mouth agape. "You can talk to dogs!"

No point denying it now, but old habits clung like white dog hairs to black jeans. "I need to get to the fairgrounds."

"So I heard."

"You're okay here?"

"I've got to leave by 3."

"I'll find someone to relieve you. Thanks, by the way, for coming in." Kari hadn't been able to come in for her shift and Rae had stepped in.

She nodded. "Any word on another place to relocate the center?"

My heart sank. "Not yet."

At the fairgrounds, Phoebe and I continued to bounce off each other like bumper cars—any accidental touch leading to a recoil in the other direction. Her shoulders stayed locked, her jaw a tight line. My throat ached with everything I should say but couldn't.

I had to let her anger go. In this moment, I needed to concentrate on the new batch of dogs Phoebe had brought in, trying to get their stories, matching them with the right new owners.

A little boy of about six ran toward the pens, crouched down and reached a hand through the mesh toward one the three French bulldog pups that were well enough for adoption. The pup licked at the sticky stuff all over the boy's hands. He giggled. "Mom! Mom! Can I have this puppy?"

The boy's mother, wearing a flowery Sunday-best dress, pulled him away from the pens. "Absolutely not." Her gaze connected with mine, her lips curling in disgust. "You are doing the devil's work."

The words lashed against my face as if she'd spit on me. My pulse thudded in my ears. I forced my expression to stay neutral.

She hefted the boy in her arms and left. He kicked against her, screaming that he wanted the puppy.

My gaze met Phoebe's. *See?*

She shook her head, tilting it toward the rest of the crowd around the pens. "One," she said, voice cold and distant. "Out of dozens."

She was right. Far many more people wanted to learn what the dogs wanted than condemned me for it. Maybe the trainer when I got certified all those years ago got it wrong. Maybe people knowing I could hear dogs' thoughts could prove an asset as a trainer.

The Pumpkin Festival finally came to an end. The carousel's last song played, a slow, winding waltz. The laughter that had filled the air all day faded into the hush of tired conversations. Car doors slammed. Engines started. The parking lot emptied. The scent of fried food gone stale and sugar cloyed the cool air.

In silence, Phoebe and I packed all the supplies and stacked the bins outside the booth.

I pointed at two blue bins. "I'll take these back to Grace at the Wash 'n Wags."

Phoebe nodded. "Thank you for all the dogs you helped get adopted. The results are even better than I expected."

"I'm sorry." My voice barely made it past the lump in my throat. I didn't know what to do with my hands or where to look. I just didn't want to see any more rejection in Phoebe's eyes. "I should have told you my secret before I spilled it out live on TV."

"I worked so hard to make the shelter successful."

"And I ruined it for you." I reached for Aunt Grace's bins. My hands felt clammy against the plastic sides. Despite the cold nipping at my cheeks, my armpits sweat as if it were noon on a hot July day. "What happened with the sponsors?"

"We lost two."

My stomach bottomed out, and I lost my grip on the bins. What had I done?

"But gained three."

My gaze snapped up.

"A natural dog food company. An accessory company. And a pet care products company. All local."

"That's good, right?"

"It is." Phoebe's mouth pressed into a thin line. "How's Max doing?"

"He's still hurt." He hadn't talked to me this morning. Or

asked about his guy. He'd barely eaten his breakfast, even though I'd sprinkled on some bacon bits. "What happened with Chris?"

"He took Archie home," Phoebe said. "The golden-mix puppy."

"That's a good fit."

"Once he's full grown, he'll make a great jogging companion."

I reached for the two bins again, hands curling around the handles but not lifting. "Are we okay?"

Phoebe's fingertips turned white against the plastic lid she was pressing into place. Her lips parted as if she wanted to say something, then shut. Finally, she shook her head, dark curls swinging around her shoulders. "I don't know."

The words cut deeper than I'd expected. I'd braced for anger. For dismissal.

But not for uncertainty.

Wind whistled around the small booth, stirring leaves and unease. A paper plate, left over from someone's funnel cake, skittered across the lane before slapping against my leg. Reaching for it, my fingers grazed the edge, but a gust of wind stole it away before I could grab it, sending it tumbling into the field.

Shoulders stiff, I hefted the bins in my arms, turned toward the parking lot, blinking fast. I had no one to blame but myself.

I'd had a chance to create a friendship, and I'd broken it instead.

And I had no idea how to fix the mess I'd made.

LAST NIGHT, the thought of going home to my grandmother's empty house had felt too cold, dark and lonely. So, I'd spent the night on the cot in my office at the canine center, even though we had no boarders that needed watching over. Sadie on one side, Hercules on the other. Both regaled me with a series of snores and snorts that I usually found comforting. Even Max had opted to sleep with me, curled up at my feet. He still wasn't talking to me, but I counted his presence as progress.

Not that the darkness and the quiet pressing against me made it possible to sleep. The heater, cycling on and off, rattled the vents on the floor. Yet the heat never quite reached my bones. My thoughts were a tangle of what-if knots that refused to loosen.

I'd made a mess of everything—Max, Caleb, Phoebe, Aimee, even Mom.

Living beings, I realized. Beings I cared for and hurt.

Somehow I had to make things right.

The alarm on my phone shrilled at 5:30. I must have fallen asleep because I startled upright, heart pounding. The only thing I knew for sure after that restless night was that, with my secret out, things would never go back to normal.

I took Sadie, Hercules and Max out back to do their business, icy morning air needling through my jacket. Their paws crinkled the coat of rime on the grass with each step. As they sniffed, looking for the perfect spot, my breath curled in front of me in pale wisps, disappearing into the sky. It seemed an apt metaphor for my future.

Back inside, I fed the dogs breakfast and prepared for the daycare arrivals.

At the front desk, I brought up the daycare reservation list for Monday. Five cancellations.

Not that I could blame them between the TV revelation and the imminent closing of the center, it made sense. Still, seeing the retreat in black and white was a punch to the gut.

"It's going to be a small group tomorrow," I told Sadie, and sighed. She looked up at me, her tail giving a little wag. At least the dogs still liked me.

I glanced at Max, who slept on the couch in the common area, back to me.

Six days left before I had to vacate the premises. Six days to figure out what came next. With the new center destroyed, I didn't have much hope of finding a new home.

"So, pivot," I told myself. I'd spent my life adapting, shifting, hiding who I was to protect myself. And now? I took in a long breath. I wasn't going to bend to anyone else's expectations.

This time, I would be me—without apology.

The dog-bone sign on the door rattled. The first person to walk into the center's door wasn't a client, but my mother.

I braced for another lecture about my choices. "What are you doing here?"

She held up a soft-sided cooler. "I figured you wouldn't have had time to stock up on food, so I brought you breakfast. And since you refuse to stay home as ordered by doctors, who, believe or not, know what they're talking about ..."

She pulled out a huge, foil-wrapped egg breakfast burrito. The scent of eggs, bacon and cheese hit me like a memory. Saturday mornings before Mom left for a shift at the hospital, she'd cook us a huge breakfast—as if the food coma would help Liam and me forget she had gone to care for someone else's kids. My fingers curled around the still-warm foil before I could stop myself.

At the scent of bacon, Max hopped off the couch, his nose twitching. He sat at attention at my feet, staring at the burrito as if it would magically float into his mouth. I pulled off a piece of bacon and fed it to him. He gobbled it down and stared for more.

Sadie appeared, sitting pretty for a cheese tax—her favorite treat. She swallowed the gob of melted cheese and licked her lips.

Hercules hobbled along, not wanting to be left out. His favorite? Warm eggs. I tore off a piece of scrambled egg and held it out for him. With the gentlest of nips, he took my offering.

Mom leaned her elbows on the desk, studying me as if she could read my fortune in the circles under my eyes. "So, how are you, truly?"

I took a bite of burrito, chewing, considering the usual lie. But something about the quiet concern in her voice unraveled me.

Instead of hiding the truth, I spilled it. "Not good, Mom."

She came around the desk and wrapped me in a hug.

I stiffened. My first instinct was to pull away, protect myself from her coming lecture, but my body was too tired to fight. I let myself lean into her warmth.

"What you did was brave," she murmured.

"It feels more like a beheading." My voice cracked like fine china.

"It's a chance to start fresh."

I swallowed hard. "I know."

I stepped back. "I may need to move to get that fresh start." I let my gaze roam around the room. "I have to leave here by Friday." I chucked my chin toward the computer. "People have already found other accommodations."

"Your strength has always been your training." She zipped the cooler back up. "You could go back to that."

I nodded, the words landing like stones in my chest. "With winter around the corner, that'll be tough. I don't have indoor space for classes."

"You could do privates in people's homes."

I'd thought of that. "It might not be enough to make a living."

"Or it could be more than you can handle."

I huffed a small laugh. "I love your optimism."

"I believe in you." She reached out and touched my arm so softly that I had to blink back tears.

"I remember you as a six-year-old," she said, shaking her head, "making after-school rounds of all the neighborhood dogs to check up on them. I remember you as a ten-year-old bringing home strays and teaching them manners before you found them the perfect home. I remember you as a teenager teaching a shelter dog how to open doors, then gifting that dog to the wheelchair-bound girl in your class.

"That service to the dogs, to their owners, that's your center of power. Start there. See where you land."

I'd found a way to keep saving dogs after Liam and Caleb started laughing at me for talking to dogs. I'd found a way to keep training dogs after Aimee had revealed my secret.

I could find a way now.

I exhaled and turned toward the computer, minimizing the reservations window and opening a new document.

Mom tilted her head. "What are you doing?"

I gave her a small smile. "Starting where I've landed."

I typed, "Lark's Mobile Dog Training" at the top of the page.

Then I made a list:

Services: Private training, Good Canine Citizen coaching, behavioral consultations, puppy basics, therapy dog prep.

Locations: In-home visits, parks, virtual sessions for follow-ups.

Start-up Needs: Training supplies, marketing plan, postcards to leave at the Wash 'n Wags, Dr. Ava's and the feed store. Referrals.

First Steps: Contact past clients, update website, announce the new business model.

The words filled the screen, and with them, something inside me clicked into place.

I wasn't just surviving. I was moving forward.

Maybe, for the first time, I was finally stepping into exactly who I was meant to be.

29

———

On Monday, while Bo played with the dogs, I worked on my new website. The center was too quiet with only a few daycare dogs around. The absence of a pack of them playing pressed into me like a missing heartbeat. The interior felt hollow, already empty even though we still had five days left in the space.

The front door opened with a tentative creak. A woman stepped inside, hesitating just past the threshold. Late thirties, maybe early forties. She had kind eyes and a guarded expression, and deep grooves of pain around her mouth. She looked around the way people did when they weren't sure if they belonged.

"Hi," I said, saving my work. "Can I help you?"

The woman glanced around at the photos of happy dogs on the wall, as if unsure she was in the right place. "I—I heard about you. The ... dog whisperer." She winced at her words as if they tasted wrong. "Sorry. That sounded—"

"No worries. I kind of like it, although I think it's already copyrighted."

The woman exhaled, nodding. "I wasn't sure if you'd still be open."

"I'm ... figuring things out. Do you have a dog that needs daycare or training?"

The woman smoothed her hands over her sleeves as if she were suddenly cold. "I don't actually have a dog. Not anymore. I just—" She stopped, her throat moving as if the words were too large. "My daughter had one. A yellow Lab. She passed away six months ago. My daughter, I mean. The dog was her service dog. Seizure alert. I didn't feel right keeping him when someone else could benefit from his training."

Service dogs had a special place in my heart. "I'm so sorry for your loss."

She glanced at the photos on the wall once again. "I've been thinking about maybe getting a dog of my own." She closed her eyes, the weight of her grief thickening the air. "I'm just not sure if I'm ... ready."

Loss—raw and quiet—hung between us. I didn't know the pain of losing a daughter, but I did understand loss. I knew what it was like to want something and not know if you deserved it.

I should say something. Tell her how a dog could help her overcome her grief. But instead, what came out was, "What was her name?"

The woman's lips parted slighting before pressing together. When she spoke, her voice was brittle, as if the edge of her grief had sharpened. "Sophia. She was the light of my life."

"That's a beautiful name."

A small smile curved her lips before it vanished. "I don't know why I came here." She shrugged, her gaze looking lost once more. "I guess I just wanted ... to be somewhere where there were dogs. Something good. Like Benny was."

"The shelter at the other end of town is always looking for

volunteers to walk and pet dogs, if you're not ready to own one quite yet."

"I hadn't thought of that."

I looked down the hall at the daycare dogs snoozing in the common area, the toys scattered from a morning of playtime. Bo spread out on the recliner, studying. Then I spotted Sadie curled up against a pillow on the couch.

"You know," I came around the desk, moving with a certainty I hadn't felt much lately, but had learned to trust. "I do have a couple of special-needs dogs, looking for a foster home." I smiled, feeling something shift inside me. "Come with me, there's someone I'd like you to meet."

The woman's fingers wrapped around the strap of her purse, gripping it tight, as if that could hold her together. "I wouldn't want to impose."

"You aren't." I waved her closer, my heart lighter than it had been in weeks. I was helping her, yes, but I was also reclaiming something, too—my place in this world.

She took a tentative step forward. I led her to the couch where Sadie lay. She cracked an eye open. Then, miracles of miracles, her tail wagged at this stranger—as if she knew this woman's need for her company was greater than Sadie's own fear.

We kneeled next to the couch. "This is Sadie," I said, voice soft and low. "She was abused by her previous owner."

I stroked Sadie's fawn-colored side, fingers bumping over the ridges of her healed scars. "She's been so afraid of everyone since she arrived that finding her a good home has been impossible. And with the center closing, I don't want to send her back to the shelter. That would be too much chaos for her. She needs quiet. She needs care." I smiled at the woman, seeing longing in her eyes. "She needs love."

"I don't know." The woman's eyes filled with fear.

"Look," I said, sensing just how much love this woman had

to give, "she's sniffing you. Do you know what she usually does when she meets a stranger?"

The woman shook her head, her uncertainty clear. She reached out to Sadie.

"She usually runs and hides under furniture and shakes like crazy. It takes me hours to get her to come back out."

The woman's hand trembled as she let Sadie sniff her palm. And when she scratched Sadie beneath her jaw, Sadie rumbled her pleasure, nuzzling deeper into the woman's touch.

These two belonged together. The sense of certainty hit me like a flash of sunlight breaking through clouds. They would heal each other. Sadie deserved that. And so did this woman, mourning her child. The joy of knowing I was making the right call filled my heart.

I hurried to the front desk and scribbled my phone number on a piece of paper, then returned to the couch. "Just think about it."

I handed her the paper. She took it carefully, running her fingers over the numbers, tracing them as if they were a lifeline. She nodded and got up.

As she left, I knew she'd return, if not later today, then before the end of the week.

After she was gone, the silence returned. But the space didn't feel quite as hollow anymore. I appreciated now that this center had meant a safe place full of life, not just for the dogs, but also for me over the past year, even if its future existence in another form was uncertain.

THAT EVENING, after closing the center, I headed for the shelter. I hesitated at the door, the frigid air nipping at my hand as I gripped the handle. Inside, the familiar din of barking dogs echoed through the building, loud and sharp. The overhead lights flickered with a sterile buzz, casting long, harsh shadows across the stained concrete. I'd spent a lot of time in this place over the years, volunteering, then taking dogs home to train and rehome.

Over the past five years, Phoebe had worked hard to keep the place open and to welcome every dog in need of a home. But as hard as she worked, even she couldn't do everything. And like me, she had a hard time keeping help. For all the good this place did, it also held a lot of sadness, and few people could deal with that unrelenting cycle of despair that felt trapped in the walls.

The least I could do now that my center was all but closed was to give Phoebe a hand.

As I entered the building, the scent of disinfectant and kibble wrapped around me—comforting in its familiarity. Phoebe sat at the front desk, hunched over a sea of paperwork, a giant travel mug of coffee cradled in one hand, the other moving in quick strokes across a clipboard. Her hair was piled in a messy bun, loose curls forming a soft halo around her tired face.

She didn't look up right away.

"Why are you here?" she asked, gaze still on her work.

"Volunteering." I shifted my weight from one foot to the other. "After this weekend, I figured you could use a little help."

She snorted. "Why should I trust you?"

I flinched. "You're right. I screwed up. And I don't know how to fix it." I got now, the redemption Aimee had sought, that my hurt had kept from her. "But I'd like a chance to try."

Phoebe blinked as if she hadn't expected the admission.

I dragged a hand through my hair, knots stopping my fingers' movement. "I've spent so long convincing myself that people will turn on me if I let them close. I was protecting myself. But all that did was push people away before they had a chance to prove me wrong."

Phoebe was quiet for a long moment. "You really think I would've turned my back on you?"

"I—I should have given you the chance to decide for yourself."

She went back to her work, pen racing across the page.

I swallowed. "This woman stopped by this morning. She wanted to be around dogs, so I told her you were always looking for volunteers."

"Umpf."

"Her daughter had a service dog, so she felt she couldn't keep the dog after her daughter died, even though it was the only thing she had left."

Phoebe frowned, still focused on her work. "Why are you telling me this sad story?"

"It reminded me how much I like to train service dogs, how there are always dogs that come through here that could make good service dogs."

That made her look up. Her eyes were sharp, measuring. "So, this is a recruitment trip?"

I winced. "I *want* to help. But if you thought someone might be a good candidate ..."

She placed her travel mug on the scuffed desk and crossed her arms. "I watched the interview again. All the way through. You did mention the shelter, so for that, I'm thankful."

She reached beneath the counter and tossed me a pair of work gloves.

Then with a sigh, she gestured toward the kennels. "Look, I'm still mad at you. But I I'm not going to say no to help. If you want to volunteer to shovel out kennels, then who I am to stop you? You can start with kennel 6—someone new came in and barfed all over the place. I was finishing up the paperwork first, but it you're volunteering ..."

"Thanks."

"Don't make me regret it."

As I turned toward the kennels, she said, "I may have a candidate for you. Kennel 9. A shepherd mix. He's goofy, but smart. He might be worth a look."

Warmth crept over my chest.

"I'll check him out after I clean 6."

Phoebe didn't smile. But the corner of her mouth twitched as she picked up the roster of new arrivals and headed toward her office.

30

———

The floor of the common room smelled like bleach and goodbye. I sat cross-legged on the cold linoleum floor in the middle of the empty room, picking at the sticker path of paw prints leading to the playrooms. Not that it mattered; the place would soon be demolished. The walls were stripped bare, showing the pale outlines where the corkboards used to hang. The couch was gone. The toys and training tools all packed in boxes, waiting for me to put them in my car. So little to show for all the work I'd done here.

The silence pressed in. Too loud. Too final.

Behind me, nails clicked on the linoleum floor—Max, fifteen pounds of terrier, a hundred pounds of ego—pacing like a coach on the sidelines at a critical moment in the game, his rough coat bristling against the cardboard boxes sealed with blue tape.

"*He's coming.*" Max barked, a soft sound as if he were trying to whisper. "*I can smell him. Scared. But he's mine.*"

"Max, please don't start." My voice cracked from disuse over the past few days and sleeplessness. "Not today."

"*Today* especially. *He needs me. It's not my fault he's slow on the uptake.*"

The front door creaked. I didn't move, but Max froze, then turned his whole body like a compass snapping north.

"Hey," Caleb said as he entered the common room.

Max barked a hello and wagged his tail hard enough to move his rear end from side to side.

I glanced over my shoulder. Caleb held two coffees, wearing the same silver reflective jacket that seemed to be his uniform since coming back home. He hadn't shaved. His gaze was hesitant. The kind of look people gave when they showed up not knowing if they were wanted.

"Didn't expect you," I said, trying to keep my voice even.

"Yeah, well." He held out one cup. "You shouldn't be alone today."

I took the take-out cup he offered and wrapped both hands around it, as if the warmth could ground me.

"The quiet," I said in a whisper, "it's so eerie."

With my nails, I picked at the edge of a blue paw print sticker, rolled the sticky vinyl into a ball. "I figured if I came early enough, I could pretend it wasn't over, that daycare dogs would show up soon."

"How's that working out?"

I gave him a weak smile. "Not great."

Caleb lowered himself to the ground next to me. Max darted forward like a heat-seeking missile and planted himself squarely on Caleb's feet, as if that would keep the man anchored.

"Really?" Caleb said to Max.

I gave him a tired smile. "You're his mission."

Caleb groaned, but didn't move. "Still?"

"*Not a phase.*" Max snorted. "*It's destiny. Also, your shoes smell like bacon. I'm never leaving.*"

"He thinks you're avoiding him." I took another slip of lukewarm coffee. "The responsibility. So he's planting himself on you."

"I'm ..." He trailed off, staring at something on the floor. "I can't have anyone needing me."

"Yeah." My voice went low. My spine curled forward as if it could no longer hold the weight of all my failures. "So you said."

Max leaned into Caleb's legs like a sandbag holding back a flood. *"Let it happen, man. Resistance is futile."*

I sipped my coffee—cream, no sugar, just like I liked it. "It's not too late for you to adopt him, you know."

Caleb shifted, but Max rode the current. "It's too much pressure."

"I get it." I shook my head in small arcs. "I keep thinking that if I shut the lights off fast enough, maybe I won't have to feel the center closing. Maybe the part of me that built this won't feel like it's dying."

"You're not the building."

"But I was safe inside it." I let out a laugh that scraped more than it soothed. "Out there, I'm the weird one who talks to dogs. In here, I could pretend. I could make it work in my favor. And nobody had to know."

Max shifted against Caleb's legs and let out a theatrical sigh. *"You're both disasters. You need each other. I'm the glue. Why aren't you listening?"*

"It's okay," I said. "You don't have to take him. I'm keeping him now that all my fosters got adopted." The woman had come back for Sadie the next day. And someone even adopted Hercules—an older gentleman, who wanted a slow-moving friend.

Caleb let out a long breath, twirling his cup in his hands, staring at it like an oracle. "I'm afraid. Of messing up. Of hurting him."

I tilted my head, watching him through a narrowed gaze.

"Everybody makes mistakes. He's resilient. He's been kicked. He's been abandoned. He's been tugged and pulled and dressed in doll's clothes. And he's still here. Still willing to give you a shot."

Max agreed. "*What she said.*"

Caleb brought the cup up to his lips, but didn't sip. "You were born for this, though. You know what to do because they tell you what they need."

"Some people will tell you I was born wrong, and that what I'm doing is the devil's work."

Caleb blinked. "It's a gift, Lark."

"I spent most of my life hiding what I could do. To make people feel at ease around me. To not be thought of as a freak."

"You're not a freak."

I let my gaze circle the room. "Without this place. Without the thing I built to feed the part of me that needed to help dogs ... I'm not quite sure what happens next. If I even can make something new happen."

Max huffed, curling against Caleb's ankles. "*You're not alone. I'm right here. Also, I will pee on his shoes if he tries to leave. Just sayin'.*"

Caleb didn't say anything for a while. "You know you don't have to go back to hiding just because this place is closing."

"I know. I have a sort of plan." I shrugged. "But ..."

"You're still you. You're still the one who knows what the dogs need. That doesn't go away just because you don't have a sign, or even a door."

I gave a wet, shaky laugh. "I'm not sure I can make a living working out of my car, doing privates."

"You'll figure it out."

"Yeah, I always do. One step at a time. One dog at a time."

Caleb leaned into me. "You're not alone."

Right then, with Caleb beside me and Max curled up as if

he belonged to both of us, I could almost believe in a new beginning.

I didn't know what would come next. But whatever happened, it wasn't the end. And this time, I wouldn't let myself disappear.

A SILENCE FELL BETWEEN US, soft, companionable. Caleb still sat beside me on the floor of the common room, fiddling with his empty coffee cup. Morning light, falling through the windows, dappled the floor in sunlit paw prints.

Max, still sitting on Caleb's feet, closed his eyes and pressed closer to Caleb's legs. I smiled. He was instinctively offering Caleb deep tissue therapy. Caleb's hand reached for Max's head, rubbing it slowly. His shoulders relaxed a notch.

"I—" he started, then shook his head, shoulders rising toward his ears again. His arm brushed against mine with a rasp.

"It's okay." I turned toward him, giving him my attention without crowding him. "You don't have to talk."

"I want to." He swallowed hard. "Last March. I was in a car accident. I keep telling myself it wasn't my fault." His fingertips pressed hard against the cardboard cups sides, creating dimples. "That's what everyone says, right?"

I turned my head toward him, afraid even a breath might shatter whatever fragile anguish he wanted to share.

"But it was my hands on the wheel." He looked at his hands as if they were foreign, shaking now. He put the coffee cup on the ground, then hugged his knees.

I didn't move. Didn't dare to say anything. Just let him pick his own pace—the way I would a nervous stray.

"We'd gone out to celebrate my girlfriend's promotion. Courtney. We went out to dinner with a group of her coworkers

—some fancy place with an outdoor patio, string lights and overpriced seafood." He attempted a smile. "She drank too much. They all did. And I wanted her to enjoy herself. She'd earned that promotion. I was driving, so I hadn't had a drop."

He'd toyed with his beer all through dinner that night at Bob's House, passing it from one hand to another, never taking a sip. I'd noticed, but not questioned, just put it down to the PTSD.

He rubbed his face as if he could scrub the memory from his mind. "We were heading back to her place in Seattle. She sang along to some terrible '90s pop song and tried to get me to sing, too."

He stopped. His jaw tightened.

"It was foggy and rainy, and the roads were slick, so I was driving carefully. Then ... Lights came at me out of nowhere. I swerved to avoid them. The front tires hit something—gravel, a patch of black ice, I don't know." His voice cracked. "The car spun around. The road—" He shook his head. "One second it was beneath us. The next, it was gone."

A sound escaped him—half breath, half defeat.

"The car went over the edge. Rolled. Hit a tree halfway down. That stopped the fall. But we were upside down, hanging there. Helpless." His throat bobbed. "Everything went quiet. So damn quiet."

He let out a slow, shaky breath. "My arms, my legs were pinned. My door was jammed. Every time I tried to move to free myself, the car creaked."

Elbows propped on his knees, he leaned his head forward, digging the heels of his palm into his forehead as if he could make the images in his mind disappear.

"So much blood. Her hair was soaked with it. Her head tilted too far. I thought she wasn't breathing. For hours, I thought she was dead."

His reaction to my scalp wound now made sense. It probably flashed him right back to seeing Courtney bleeding and thinking she was dead.

His hands stilled. "Couldn't reach my phone. Couldn't call for help. Couldn't really move without risking the car falling the rest of the way. I tried calling to her over and over until I was hoarse. Nothing."

Tears welled in my eyes. What a nightmare that must have been. No wonder he couldn't get in a car.

"Even when the rescue team showed up, she didn't wake up. I had them take her out first."

"Was she ...?"

He shook his head. "She was alive. Concussion. Broken rib. She got twelve stitches. She came back. Me? Only bruises."

Relief flooded through me that he didn't have her death on his conscience.

He looked down at his hands as if they were still covered with blood. "But something in me didn't."

"Caleb ..."

"After ... I couldn't touch the wheel of a car without my hands sweating and my heart pounding. I couldn't fall asleep without hearing that eerie silence, then that creak. Courtney said she couldn't deal with that. So, she left."

He gave a wry smile. "Couldn't blame her. I was there, but... not."

Max shifted his head to encourage Caleb to pet him again. Caleb complied and looked down at the small dog, giving him his all. "I haven't driven since. Haven't let myself be responsible for anyone else."

"So, when you look at Max, you see ...?"

"I see a life hanging. I keep thinking, what if something happens to him? What if I freeze? What if I fail him? That's why I can't take him. He deserves someone who doesn't wake up every night, reliving that nightmare. Someone who can act during an emergency and not freeze."

"You were pinned. If you could have reached for her, you would have. You helped me that day the ceiling fell on my head." I reached for one of his hands, twined my fingers around his. "You're not weak, Caleb. And Max *wants* the job of helping you through those nightmares."

He nodded, but it didn't feel like agreement. "My brothers keep telling me to get over myself. That it was just an accident. No one died."

"Don't listen to them. They're macho idiots." I rubbed my thumb over the back of his hand. "It wasn't just an accident. It was a major trauma."

"As volunteer firefighters, they deal with worse trauma."

"But they're not you. They don't have a heart as big as yours. And you're still healing. Max knows that and wants to be there for you."

"I—"

"Max deserves love. And you already love him. If you didn't, you wouldn't care what happens to him."

He looked at me, gaze drilling so deeply inside of me that I could feel it in my solar plexus. He wanted to believe me.

"You didn't leave her," I said.

"I couldn't move."

"Exactly. And if you could have, you would have. You would've done everything possible to help her. Just like you did for me. That's the kind of guy you are. Have always been since I've known you."

After a moment, he stood. Our hands fell apart, and I suddenly felt unmoored.

Max circled Caleb's ankles as if he were trying to herd him home. "*Not letting you go.*"

"I almost forgot," Caleb said, a new steadiness to his voice. "I came here for a reason."

He jerked his head toward the door. "Come." He offered me his hand again—an invitation. "There's something I want to show you."

31

Outside, morning light scattered gold across the fields, catching on the neighbor's wire fencing like a wink. A lump formed in my throat as I turned the key in the lock of the canine center for the last time. The wooden, bone-shaped Welcome sign rattled against the door. I traced a finger around the faded paint along its edges from all the times it bounced when someone came in or left. I couldn't leave the sign behind to be destroyed along with the building. I unhooked it from the door, then headed for the car.

Max trotted ahead, tail wagging like a tour guide's flag, leading the way. Once at the car, he stopped and surveyed us, making sure we fell into step. *"Chop, chop,"* he barked. *"We're going home!"*

"He thinks we're going home." I lifted the station wagon's tailgate and dropped the Welcome sign on a blanket. A memento of all the good that had happened here. A sign of hope for things to come.

"Not quite yet." Caleb reached for his bike, leaning against the building's mustard-colored side and rolled it over toward me.

I started to close the hatch, but Caleb said, "Wait up. I want to put my bike back there."

I studied him, looking for what I wasn't sure. I found determination stamped on his face. "You don't have to."

"I want to."

He placed his bike in the back of the station wagon, then headed toward the passenger's side. Not panicked, but with deliberate steps. Hand on the door handle, he hesitated for half a moment, then yanked the door open and slipped into the seat.

Max jumped into the back with a happy grunt, tail thudding against the seat. "*Let's go!*"

Exhaling a breath I'd held too long, I took my place in the driver's seat. I just sat. I didn't move. I didn't speak. I let him take this step on his own terms.

Caleb let out a breath. "I'm okay."

I put the key in the ignition and let the engine idle. Then I turned to Max in the back seat, signaling for him to hop over to the front seat. "Come here."

Max was halfway over when Caleb stopped him. "Isn't that dangerous?"

"I'll drive slow. I want him there for you."

He stared at me, then nodded once. "I'll ride in the back with him."

I gave him a crooked smile. "That's going to make me feel like a chauffeur."

As he settled into the back seat, making sure to clip Max's safety belt as well as his own into place, he laughed, a soft, real sound. Max hopped onto his lap as if it was his rightful place.

I tipped my imaginary hat, then put the car in gear. He stared straight ahead, his chest rising and falling too fast.

"Where to, guv'nor?" I said in my best British accent to lighten the moment, giving him a chance to settle.

His face blanched. Max squeezed in closer. "Watching British crime shows again?"

"They're the best." I turned to look at him over my shoulder, the hum of the engine filling the car's interior. "Where am I driving to?"

"Head towards Brighton."

I nodded. Heartbeat loud in my ears, I tapped the gas, accelerating slowly. I pulled onto Thistle Hill, glancing at him in the rearview mirror.

Trees blurred past. He sat there, every muscle rigid, both hands around Max, who pressed his little body against Caleb's chest, steadying him.

My heart ached with pride for his courage, sorrow that he'd had to bear this pain for so long, and admiration for rising above his trauma. He'd made a big choice in getting into the car. He'd chosen freedom over fear. I wanted to cheer him on, but I didn't want to scare him.

He was in the car. And the car was moving. And he seemed okay.

"Where are we going?" I asked again, softly, once I reached the main road.

A crow flew overhead, its wings cutting through the sky like a streak of ink. The wind carried the scent of hay from the bales in the fields, of composting leaves, of distant smoke.

"You'll see," he said, mystery wrapped in his voice. "Turn left here."

The drive was quiet, wrapping around us like a blanket. With each roll of the tires, the weight of the past eased little by little. He kept patting Max's head as if it were his anchor.

Max gave a gentle woof. *"Now tell me we don't belong together."*

You do.

Fifteen minutes passed before he spoke again. "Slow down up here. Turn right at the split."

I drove past grazing cows, fences lined with moss, the sky streaked with white contrails. Brighton shimmered in the distance—small, quiet, familiar. But this road curved away, leading to the outskirts.

"Here," Caleb said, leaning forward, arm pointing toward an entrance flanked by a red mailbox. "Pull in."

I eased onto the gravel drive, tires crunching toward the big, red barn, surrounded by a fenced field on one side and a grove of birches on the other. Something about the weathered wood, the wide door that looked like a smile and the windows in the loft that seemed like eyes crinkled with laughter, felt like a welcome.

I turned off the engine, staring at the barn, sitting there alone with no other buildings around. "What is this place?"

Caleb scrambled out of the car, Max bounding out after him. Caleb circled to my side, breathless with excitement. "Come on."

He offered me his hand. I took it, the warmth of his fingers grounding me as my pulse ticked in my ears.

The air suddenly buzzed.

I froze.

My legs went rubbery, as if my body understood something before my mind did.

Voices, low and steady, murmuring as if coming from inside the barn. The rhythmic thunk of hammers, punctuated by the whine of a saw. Laughter carried on the breeze like music.

I looked at Caleb. "What is this?"

He didn't answer, but a wide smile spread over his face.

"Is it yours?" I asked, confused.

He shook his head. "No, yours."

"Mine?" The word didn't make sense. I stared at the barn, at the stir of activity inside. My chest went tight, leaving me feeling raw and exposed. "I don't understand."

"I bought it for you."

"Caleb, no—I can't accept this."

"Why not?"

"Because … it's too much." My voice cracked.

"Everybody you've helped in the past is here for you. They're helping convert the barn into your new canine center."

"But I didn't ask—"

"They want to do it, Lark. That's why they're here. Because you never ask. It's for all you've done for their animals. For all the happiness you've added to their lives by making sure they took the right dog home."

The barn doors flew open.

"She's here!" someone yelled.

Inside the barn, at least two dozen people stared at me. I knew them all. Aimee and Oliver. Phoebe. My cousins Aaron, Maeve and Zoe. My parents. My aunt and uncle. Bo, Rae and Kari. Chris from the Adopt-a-Thon who'd adopted Archie. Past clients. New owners.

Children and dogs ran around in the outside play pens—one for smaller dogs and one for bigger dogs. Happy sounds of laughter and barks filled the air.

Neve ran forward, holding a freshly painted sign with purple glitter. "Welcome," was written on a bone-shaped sheet of paper. Just like the sign I'd placed in the car earlier.

My breath stuttered. I pressed a hand to my chest to hold all the emotions back. "What are they all doing here?"

"Sleep suites." Caleb placed a hand on my lower back and pressed me forward into the barn's center concrete aisleway. "Play areas. A common space. An office. A kitchenette-slash-grooming corner. And an apartment upstairs in the loft."

"It's–" My throat closed. I couldn't speak. I looked at all of them. Pride shown in their eyes. Joy. "Too much."

"It's not enough." He wrapped an arm around my shoulders and pulled me closer, planting a kiss on top of my head. "You deserve this."

I blinked against the tears slipping down my cheeks. Taking in the scene of people working, dogs playing, children laughing, rinsed away the last remnant of this morning's grief. "I don't know what to say."

Caleb smiled against my hair. "It's customary to say thank you."

I turned to him, my voice rough. "Thank you."

32

———

In the barn, the scent of fresh sawdust and old hay hung in the air, sweetened by the late-afternoon sun slanting through the open doors. I stood just inside the threshold, blinking back tears as person after person stopped to hug me, share a story, thank me.

I spotted Phoebe, directing the hanging of a whiteboard behind the reception desk.

I went to stand next to her. "You're here."

"You sound surprised."

"After the way we left things ... I wasn't sure where we stood."

"Yeah, well, sometimes I let my feelings get hurt. Never a good thing." She signaled the guys holding the white board to lift it higher. "I got over myself. You did what you did for the dogs. And I'm in the business of second chances, after all."

A second chance. The thought brought tears to my eyes. I was tearing up too much today. "Thank you."

She shrugged one shoulder in a no-big-deal way. But it was a big deal. "Still on for the paint-and-sip on next weekend?"

"You still want me to go?"

"Of course. Those things are no fun by yourself."

"Then, yes, I'd love to go."

"Hey!" Phoebe called to the man hammering in a hook. "You're making it crooked!"

She stomped in their direction to show them the right way.

Aimee stood by the entrance to the sleep suites, smiling, one hand holding a paintbrush, the other petting Bubbles' head as if they'd always been together. Kids darted around the play rooms with dogs trailing after them, while adults mingled and worked on the new sleep suites. Someone handed me a glass of lemonade. Someone else pressed a folded note into my palm. My heart ached in the best of ways, full, so full.

"Hey," I said, drifting over to where Aimee stood, tucking a strand of hair behind my ear. "Didn't expect to see you wielding a paintbrush."

"I'll have you know I'm quite skilled at manual labor, thank you very much."

I laughed. "I mean it. Thank you. For today. For stepping up to adopt Bubbles. For not giving up on me."

Aimee's gaze softened. "I did some giving up back then, too. It hurt when you wouldn't talk to me. Going away seemed the easier choice. But I missed home. I missed you." Bubbles spied Oliver and went hopping to him. "When I met Oliver, you were the first person I wanted to call."

I got that. "So many times, I picked up the phone to call you."

We shared a smile, the kind that felt like spring after a long, bitter winter.

She lifted her paintbrush. "I better get back to it. What are you doing tomorrow night?"

"I'm not sure."

"You and Caleb should come over for dinner at the house."

The kind of evening Aimee had talked about when we were

kids, dreaming about when we'd have boyfriends, husbands and eventually kids. "I'd like that."

Her smile could have lit the whole barn.

As dusk painted the sky in strokes of lavender and coral, Caleb approached, Max trotting on his heels.

"Can I steal you for a minute?" he asked.

"You already have."

We walked along the fence line, Max sniffing every post for coded messages.

The breeze ruffled Caleb's hair and carried the hum of laughter and barking from the barn.

"All this," I said, pointing to the barn. "It was your idea?"

"Theirs. I ran into Aimee at the store, and she said she'd found the perfect space for you but that it was out of your budget. I asked her to show it to me and made an offer."

"Just like that."

"Just like that. She's the one who came up with the conversion idea and rounded up the supplies and people to do it."

"She can be a force of nature." Even after everything I'd put her through. Another reason for me to thank her.

I stopped walking. My gaze met his. "I'm scared," I said. "It's all ... so much. So fast. And—" I scooped in a breath as if there wasn't enough air in all the outdoors. "I like you. And that scares me."

"I know. Me, too." He took my hands in his and drew me closer. "Chances are, things with me are going to be rocky for a while."

"You have Max. And me. That's a start."

He smiled. "I was going to say that together, we can do anything."

Max trotted up to us, plopped on the grass at our feet and gave a satisfied sigh. "*About time.*"

"I want to try. Not just with this new center. With you. With Max. With everything."

His forehead brushed mine. "Then let's start now. To show you I mean what I say, I'm going to step up and adopt Max."

His kiss was gentle, not rushed. The kind of kiss that said we had all the time in the world.

When we pulled apart, Max wagged his tail, smug as could be. "*I knew it all along.*"

We both laughed.

As we headed back to the barn and the picnic waiting there, the world seemed warm and alive despite the cold October air.

The future didn't seem so bleak and scary anymore.

The barn, the community, the dogs, Caleb ... it all felt like home.

Authors depend on word of mouth. So, if you have time, I'd be grateful if you would post a short review on Amazon, Goodreads, BookBub or wherever you bought the book.

All the best,
Sylvie

Want to keep up with what's going on in Brighton Village? Join my VIP Readers List today. The newsletter comes out (more or less) once a month and contains book updates, behind the scenes tidbits, recipes, specials and extras only my VIP readers receive. Go to https://sylviekurtz.com/newsletter and sign up now!

MAEVE'S RASPBERRY BROWNIES

In *Rescue You*, Lark asks Maeve for brownies as payment for watching Neve during an unexpected school day off, mostly as a way to mask her own inability to say no. These brownies are nice and fudgy and taste sinfully rich.

Ingredients:

- ¾ cup unsalted butter, melted
- ¾ unsweetened cocoa powder
- 1 teaspoon vanilla
- 1-3/4 cup light brown sugar
- 3 large eggs
- ¾ cup flour
- ½ teaspoon salt
- ½ cup fresh raspberries (you can also use still frozen berries)
- ½ cup dark chocolate chips

Instructions:

1. Preheat the oven to 350°F. Grease and line an 8 X 8-inch pan with parchment paper.
2. In a large bowl, whisk melted butter, cocoa, and vanilla together until no cocoa lumps remain.
3. In a mixer fitted with a whisk attachment, beat the eggs and brown sugar until light and fluffy.
4. Fold the butter mixture into the egg mixture.
5. Fold the flour and salt into the mixture until no trace of flour remains.
6. Gently fold in the raspberries (if using frozen raspberries, keep them frozen so they don't crumble apart) and chocolate chips.
7. Transfer the mixture into the prepared pan. Bake for about 25 minutes until a knife inserted into the center comes out with a bit of brownie batter. If you're using frozen raspberries, the brownies will take a bit more time to bake.

BOOK CLUBS
LET'S MEET!

Is your book club planning to read one of my books? I love to talk with readers. If you would like me to visit your book club, a 30-minute online or phone visit with your club is always free.

Just use my contact form to let me know about your gathering, or if you have any questions about how it works.

Can't wait to chat!

P.S. You can find readers' guides for each book in the "Love in Brighton Village" series at: https://sylviekurtz.com/for-readers.

READERS' GUIDE FOR

RESCUE YOU, LOVE IN BRIGHTON VILLAGE
BOOK 5

1. Because of bad experiences as a girl, Lark feels the need to keep the fact that she can hear dogs a secret. What secret have you felt you needed to hide? Why?
2. Dogs mean the world to Lark. They're her reason for getting up every morning. Do you own a dog? How have they enriched your life? What's your reason for getting up in the morning?
3. Caleb feels the need to hide his PTSD because the trauma he suffered is considered no big deal by others. He feels broken because he can't just get over it. How has trauma affected your life, or the life of someone you know?
4. Making friends as an adult is difficult, especially when you're used to being an outsider. What do you think makes a good friend? Where are the best places to meet new friends as an adult?
5. Lark and Aimee had a falling out in high school. Lark feels Aimee betrayed her for a chance to be part of the "it" girls. How do Lark and Aimee

navigate their relationship after Aimee returns to
Brighton? Can a friendship truly survive a betrayal?
6. What do you think Lark has learned about
friendship through dealing with Aimee, Caleb and
Phoebe?

Download the guide for *Rescue You* online and get additional
ideas to host a dog-themed get-together.

ACKNOWLEDGMENTS

Writing is a solitary pursuit and it's nice to have people on the sidelines cheering, especially when things go wrong. Thank you to everyone who's been there for me this past year through all the ups and downs of two surgeries and all the recovery time that required. Asking for help is never easy.

As always, thank you, dear reader, for choosing to spend time in the fictional world of Brighton Village and its many festivals. I hope these stories continue to bring a smile and some joy to your world.

ALSO BY SYLVIE KURTZ

Love in Brighton Village Series

Christmas by Candlelight

Christmas in Brighton

Summer's Sweet Spot

The Christmas Star

Rescue You

Brighton Village Cozy Mystery

Of Books and Bones (novella)

Midnight Whispers Series

One Texas Night

Blackmailed Bride

Hidden Legacy

Alyssa Again

Beneath the Surface

Darker Than Night

Pull of the Moon

Remembering Red Thunder

Red Thunder Reckoning

Into the Fire

Detour

The Seekers Series

Heart of a Hunter

Mask of a Hunter

Eye of a Hunter

Pride of a Hunter

Spirit of a Hunter

Honor of a Hunter

Action-Adventure Romance

Ms. Longshot

Paranormal Romance

Broken Wings

Silver Shadows

Holiday Romance

A Little Christmas Magic

ABOUT THE AUTHOR

Sylvie writes stories that celebrate family, friends and food. She believes organic dark chocolate is an essential nutrient, likes to knit with soft yarn, and justifies watching movies that require a box of tissues, and by knitting baby blankets. She has written 27 novels in various genres.

Her first Harlequin Intrigue, *One Texas Night*, was a 1999 Romantic Times nominee for Best First Category Romance and a finalist for a Booksellers Best Award. Her Silhouette Special Edition, *A Little Christmas Magic* was a 2001 Readers' Choice Award Finalist and a Waldenbooks bestseller. *Remembering Red Thunder* was a 2002 Romantic Times Nominee for Best Intrigue. *Broken Wings* was an RWA Golden Heart finalist. She was a 2005, 2007 and 2008 Romantic Times nominee for Lifetime Achievement for Series Romantic Adventure. Twin Star Entertainment optioned *Ms. Longshot* as a possible TV movie.

For more details, visit https://sylviekurtz.com.

facebook.com/sylviekurtzauthor

instagram.com/sylviekurtzauthor